THE MAID'S
SPANISH SECRET

THE MAID'S
SPANISH SECRET

DANI COLLINS

MILLS & BOON

First published in Great Britain 2019
by Mills & Boon, an imprint of HarperCollins*Publishers*
1 London Bridge Street, London, SE1 9GF

Large Print edition 2019

© 2019 Dani Collins

ISBN: 978-0-263-08304-0

MIX
Paper from
responsible sources
FSC® C007454

This book is produced from independently certified FSC™ paper to ensure responsible forest management. For more information visit www.harpercollins.co.uk/green.

Printed and bound in Great Britain
by CPI Group (UK) Ltd, Croydon, CR0 4YY

For my editor, Laurie Johnson,
and the wonderful team at
Harlequin Mills & Boon in London.

Romance novels taught me
to chase my dreams, and writing
for Mills & Boon Modern Romance
was a lifelong goal.

Thirty books in, I'm still astonished
and eternally grateful that you've
made this dream come true for me.

Thank you.

PROLOGUE

Rico Montero arrived at his brother's villa, two hours up the coast from Valencia, in seventy-three minutes. He'd been feeling cooped up in his penthouse, hungry for air. He had pulled his GTA Spano out of storage and tried to escape his own dark mood, not realizing the direction he took until he was pulled over for speeding.

Recognizing where he was, he told the officer he was on his way to see his brother— a means of name-dropping the entire family. The ploy had gotten him out of having his license suspended, but he still had to pay a fine.

Since he was literally in the neighborhood, he decided not to compound his crimes by lying. He rolled his way through Cesar's vineyard to the modern home sprawled against a hillside.

He told himself he didn't miss the vineyard he had owned with pride for nearly a decade—long before his brother had decided he had an interest in grapes and winemaking. Rico's fascination with the process had dried up along with his interest in life in general. Selling that property had been a clean break from a time he loathed to dwell upon.

It's been eighteen months, his mother had said over lunch yesterday. *Time to turn our attention to the future.*

She had said something similar three months ago and he had dodged it. This time, he sat there and took the bullet. *Of course. Who did you have in mind?*

He had left thinking, *Go ahead and find me another scheming, adulterous bride.* But he hadn't said it aloud. He had promised to carry that secret to his grave.

For what?

He swore and jammed the car into Park,

then threw himself out of it, grimly aware he had completely failed to escape his dour mood.

"Rico!" His sister-in-law Sorcha opened the door before he had climbed the wide steps. She smiled with what looked like genuine pleasure and maybe a hint of relief.

"Mateo, look. Tío Rico has come to see you." She spoke to the bawling toddler on her hip. "That's a nice surprise, isn't it?"

She wasn't the flawlessly elegant beauty he was used to seeing on Cesar's arm, more of a welcoming homemaker. Her jeans and peasant-style top were designer brands, but she wore minimal makeup and her blond hair was tied into a simple ponytail. Her frown at her unhappy son was tender and empathetic, not the least frazzled by his tantrum.

The deeply unhappy Mateo pointed toward the back of the house. "*Ve*, Papi."

"He's overdue for his nap." Sorcha waved Rico in. "But he knows *someone* took *someone else* into the V-I-N-E-Y-A-R-D."

"You're speaking English and you still have to spell it out?" Rico experienced a glimmer of amusement.

"He's picking it up *so* fast. Oh!" She caught Mateo as he reached out to Rico, nearly launching himself from her arms.

Rico caught him easily while Sorcha stammered, "I'm sorry."

If Rico briefly winced in dismay, it was because of the look in Sorcha's eyes. Far too close to pity, it contained sincere regret that her son was prevailing on him for something she thought too big and painful to ask.

It wasn't. The favor he was doing for his former in-laws was a greater imposition, spiking far more deeply into a more complex knot of nerves. What Sorcha thought she knew about his marriage was the furthest thing from reality.

And what she read as pain and anger at fate was contempt and fury with himself for being a fool. He was steeped in bitterness, playing a role that was barely a version of the truth. A version that made a sensitive soul like Sorcha wear a poignant smile as she gazed on him holding his young nephew.

Mateo stopped crying, tears still on his cheeks.

"*Ve*, Papi?" he tried.

The tyke had been born mere weeks before Rico's ill-fated marriage. Mateo was sturdy and stubborn and full of the drive that all the Montero males possessed. This was why he was giving his mother such a hard time. He knew what he wanted and a nap wouldn't mollify him.

"We'll discuss it," he told the boy and glanced at Sorcha. "You should change," he advised, unable to bear much more of that agonized happiness in her eyes.

"Why—? Ugh." She noticed the spot where Mateo had rubbed his streaming face against her shoulder. "You're okay?" she asked with concern.

"For God's sake, Sorcha," he muttered through clenched teeth.

He regretted his short temper immediately and quickly reined in his patience. His secret sat in him like a cancer, but he couldn't let it provoke him into lashing out, certainly not at the nicest person in his family.

"I didn't mean to speak so sharply," he managed to say, gathering his composure as he brought his nephew to his shoulder. "We're fine."

"It's okay, Rico." She squeezed his arm. "I understand."

No. She didn't. But thankfully she disappeared, leaving him to have a man-to-man chat with Mateo, who hadn't forgotten a damned thing. He gave it one more try, pointing and asking for Cesar, who had taken his older brother Enrique to speak to winemakers and pet cellar cats and generally have a barrel of a good time by anyone's standards.

Mateo's eyes were droopy, his cheeks red, very much worn out from his tantrum.

"I know what you're going through," he told the boy. "Better than you can imagine."

Like Mateo, Rico was the younger brother to the future *duque*. He, too, occupied the unlit space beneath the long shadow of greatness cast by the heir. He, too, was expected to live an unblemished life so as not to tarnish the title he would never hold. Then there was the simple, fraternal rivalry of a brother being that few years older and moving into the next life stage. Envy was natural, not that Monteros were allowed to feel such things. Emotions were too much like pets, requiring regular feeding and liable to leave a mess on the floor.

Rico climbed the grand staircase to the bedroom that had been converted to a playroom for the boys, not dwelling on Cesar's stellar fulfillment of his duty with two bright and healthy children, a beautiful home and a stunning, warmhearted wife.

"There are some realities that are not worth crying about," he informed Mateo as they entered the room. "Your father told me that." It was one of Rico's earliest memories.

Cry all you want. They won't care. Cesar had spoken with the voice of experience after Rico had been denied something he'd desperately wanted that he could no longer recollect.

Cesar had come to reason with him, perhaps because he was tired of having his playmate sent into solitary confinement. Reason was a family skill valued far more highly than passion. Reason was keeping him silent and carrying on today, maintaining order rather than allowing the chaos that would reign if the truth came out.

Doesn't it make you mad that they won't even listen? Rico had asked Cesar that long-ago day.

Yes. Cesar had been very mature for a boy of six or seven. *But getting mad won't change anything. You might as well accept it and think about something else.*

Words Rico had learned to live by.

He was capable of basic compassion, however.

"I'll always listen if you need to get something off your chest," he told his nephew as he lowered them both into an armchair. "But sometimes there's nothing to be done. It's a hard fact of life, young man."

Mateo wound down to sniffling whimpers.

He decided to explore Rico's empty chest pocket.

"Should we read a book?" Rico picked up the first picture book within reach. It was bilingual, with trains and dogs and bananas labeled in English and Spanish.

As he worked through the pages, he deliberately pitched his voice to an uninflected drone. The boy's head on his chest grew heavier and heavier.

"Thank you," Sorcha whispered when she peeked in.

Rico nodded and carried the sleeping boy to his crib. The nanny came in with the baby monitor.

Rico followed Sorcha down the stairs saying, "I'll go find Cesar. If Mateo wakes, don't tell him what a traitor I am."

"Actually, I was going to invite you for dinner later this week. There's something I want to talk to you about. Can we go into Cesar's office?" Her brow pleated with concern.

Rico bit back a sigh, trying to hold on to the temper that immediately began to slip.

"If this is about me remarrying, Mother has passed along your concerns."

Your sister-in-law thinks it's too soon, his mother had said yesterday, not asking him how *he* felt. She had merely implied that in Sorcha's view, he was in a weakened state. His choice had been to confirm it or go along with his mother's insistence on finding him a new wife.

"This is something else," Sorcha murmured, closing the door and waving toward the sofa. "And my imagination could be running wild. I haven't said anything to Cesar."

She poured two glasses of the Irish whiskey she had turned Cesar on to drinking and brought one to where Rico stood.

"Really?" he drawled, wondering what she could possibly impart that would need to be absorbed with a bracing shot. He left the whiskey on the end table as they both sat.

"Please don't be angry with me. I know I was overstepping, suggesting your mother hold off on pressing you to remarry, but I care about all of you." She sat with her elbows on her thighs, leaning forward, hands clasped. "You may not be the most demonstrative family, but you *are* family. I will never stay silent if I think one of you needs…" Her mouth tightened.

"Sorcha." He meticulously gathered his forbearance. "I'm fine." And, before he had to suffer another swimming gaze of tormented sympathy, he added, "If I were in your shoes, I would understand why you think I'm not, but honestly, you have to stop worrying about me."

"That's never going to happen," she said primly, which would have been endearing if he didn't find it so frustratingly intrusive. "And there may be other factors to consider." She sipped her drink and eyed him over it. Then sighed. "I feel like such a hypocrite."

He lifted his brows. "Why? What's going on?"

She frowned, set down her drink and picked up her phone, stared at it without turning it on. "Elsa, our nanny, showed me something that came up in her news feed."

"Something compromising?" Sorcha would have taken up the concern with Cesar unless— Oh, hell. Had something gotten out from the coroner's report? "Is this about Faustina?" His molars ground together on reflex.

"No! No, it's not about her at all." She touched her brow. "Elsa always comes with us when we have dinner at your mother's. She's acquainted with the maids there and follows some of them online."

At the word *maid* a premonition danced in his periphery. He refused to reach for the drink, though. It would be a tell. Instinctively, he knew he had to maintain impassivity. He couldn't tip his hand. Not before he knew exactly what was coming next.

"To be honest, I rarely check my social media accounts," he said with a disinterested brush of non-existent lint from his knee. "Especially since Faustina passed. It's very maudlin."

"I suppose it would be." Her expression grew pinched. She looked at the phone she held pressed between her palms. "But one way or another, I think you should be aware of this particular post."

Biting her lips together, she touched her thumb to the sensor and the screen woke. She flicked to bring up a photo and held it out to him.

"On first glance, Elsa thought it was Mateo dressed up as a girl. That's the only reason she took notice and showed me. She thought it was funny that it had given her a double take. I had to agree this particular photo offers a certain resemblance."

Rico flicked a look at the toddler. He'd never seen Mateo in a pink sailor's bib and hat, but the baby girl's grin was very similar, minus a few teeth, to the one he had coaxed out of his nephew before the boy's head had drooped against his chest.

"I actually keep my privacy settings locked down tight," Sorcha said. "I've heard photos can be stolen and wind up in ads without permission. I thought that's what had happened. Elsa assured me she never shares images of the boys with anyone but me or Cesar."

The Montero fortune had been built on the development of chemicals and special alloys. Rico had learned early that certain substances, innocuous on their own, could become explosive when in proximity to one another.

Sorcha was pouring statements into beakers before him. A maid. A baby that looked like other children in the family.

He wouldn't let those two pieces of information touch. Not yet.

"It's said we all have a double." His lifetime of suppressing emotion served him well. "It would seem you've found Mateo's."

"This is the only photo where she looks so much like him," Sorcha murmured, taking back her phone. "I looked up the account. Her mother is a photographer."

Photographer. One beaker began to tip into another.

"This is part of her portfolio for her home business. Her name is Poppy Harris. The mother, I mean. The baby is Lily."

His abdomen tightened to brace for a kick.

A sizzle resounded in his ears. Adrenaline made him want to reach for his drink, but he only lifted his hand to scratch his cheek—while his mind conjured the forest of lilies that had surrounded them in his mother's solarium as he and Poppy had made love so impulsively.

"Do you...remember her?" Sorcha asked tentatively.

Skin scented like nectarines, lush corkscrews of curly red hair filling his hands as he consumed her crimson lips. He remembered the exact pitch of her joyful cries of release, the culmination of madness like he'd never known before or since.

And he remembered vividly the ticking of the clock on the mantel as he had sat in his mother's parlor the next morning, an itchy fire in his blood driving him mad. He'd been on the verge of going to look for her because he couldn't stop thinking about her.

Then Faustina had arrived, striking like dry lightning with sheepishly delivered news. Family obligation had crashed upon him afresh, pinning him under the weight of a wedding that had been called off, but now was back on. They would pretend the gap in the parade had never happened.

"Rico?" Sorcha prompted gently, dragging him back to the present. "I know this must be a shock." And there was that infernal compassion again.

He swore, tired to his *bones* of people thinking he was mourning a baby he had already known wasn't his. He was sorry for the loss of a life before it had had the chance to start. Of course he was. But he wasn't grieving with the infinite heartbreak of a parent losing a child. It hadn't been *his*.

And given Faustina's trickery, he was damned cynical about whether he had conceived *this* one.

"Why did you jump straight to suspecting she's mine?" he asked baldly.

Sorcha was slightly taken aback. "Well, I'm not going to suspect my own husband, am I?" Her tone warned that he had better not, either. Her chin came up a notch. "You were living in your parents' villa at the time. Frankly, your father doesn't seem particularly passionate about any woman, young or old. You, however, were briefly unengaged."

Rico had long suspected the success of his parents' marriage could be attributed to both of them being fairly asexual and lacking in passion for anything beyond cool reason and the advancement of family interests.

Sorcha's eyes grew big and soft and filled with that excruciating pity. "I'm not judging, Rico. *I know how these things happen.*"

"I bet you do." He regretted it immediately. It wasn't him. At least, it wasn't the man he was beneath the layer of caustic fury he couldn't seem to shed. Sorcha certainly didn't deserve this ugly side of him. She was kind and sensitive and everything the rest of them didn't know how to be.

She recoiled, rightly shocked that he would deliver such a belly blow. But she hadn't risen above the scandal of secretly delivering his brother's baby while Cesar had been engaged

to someone else without possessing truck-
loads of resilience.

"I meant because my mother was my father's maid when she conceived *me*." Her
voice was tight and strong, but there was such
a wounded shadow in her gaze, he had to look
away and reach for the drink she'd poured
him.

He drained it, burning away the words that
hovered on his tongue. Words he couldn't
speak because he was trying to spare Faustina's parents some humiliation when they
were already destroyed by the loss of their
only child.

"I'll assume if you're lashing out, you believe it's possible that little girl is yours. How
she came about is your business, Rico, but
don't you *ever* accuse me of trapping Cesar
into this marriage. I *left*, if you recall." She
stood, hot temper well lit, but honed by her
marriage to a Montero into icy severity. "And
so did Poppy. Maybe ask yourself why, if
you're such a prize, she doesn't want any-

thing to do with you. *I* have an idea, if you can't figure it out for yourself."

She stalked to the door and swung it open, inviting him to leave using nothing more than a head held high and an expression of frosty contempt that prickled his conscience through the thick shields of indifference he had been bricking into place since Faustina had been found.

"I shouldn't have said that," Rico ground out, mind reeling so badly as he stood, his head swam. "I was shooting the messenger." With a missile launcher loaded with nuclear waste. "Tell Cesar what you've told me. I'll let him punch me in the face for what I said to you." He meant it.

She didn't thaw. Not one iota. "Deal with the message. I have a stake in the outcome, as do my husband and sons."

"Oh, I will," he promised. *"Immediately."*

CHAPTER ONE

POPPY HARRIS FILLED the freshly washed sippy cup with water only to have Lily ignore it and keep pointing at the shelf.

"You want a real cup, don't you?"

Two weeks ago, Lily's no-spill cup had gone missing from daycare. Poppy's grandmother, being old-school, thought cups with closed lids and straws were silly. Back in *her* day, babies learned to drink from a proper cup.

Since she was pinching pennies, Poppy hadn't bought a new one. She had spent days mopping dribbles instead, and she'd been *so* happy when the cup had reappeared today.

Unfortunately, Lily was a big girl now. She wanted an open cup. *Thanks, Gran.*

Poppy considered whether a meltdown right before dinner was worth the battle. She compromised by easing Lily's grip off her pant leg and then sat her gently onto her bottom, unable to resist running affectionate fingertips through Lily's fine red-gold curls. She handed her both the leakproof cup and an empty plastic tumbler. Hopefully that would keep her busy for a few minutes.

"I'm putting the biscuits in the oven, Gran," Poppy called as she did it.

She scooped a small portion of leek-and-potato soup from the slow cooker into a shallow bowl. She had started the soup when she raced home on her lunch break to check on her grandmother. Every day felt like a flat-out run, but she didn't complain. Things could be worse.

She set the bowl on the table so it would be cool enough for Lily to eat when they sat down.

"The fanciest car has just pulled in, Poppy," her grandmother said in her quavering voice. Her evening game shows were on, but she preferred to watch the comings and goings beyond their front room window. "Is he one of your models needing a head shot? He's *very* handsome."

"What?" Poppy's stomach dropped. It was completely instinctive and she made herself take a mental step back. There was no reason to believe it would be *him*.

Even so, she struggled to swallow a jagged lump that lodged in her suddenly arid throat. "Who—?"

The doorbell rang.

Poppy couldn't move. She didn't want to see. If it wasn't Rico, she would be irrationally disappointed. If it *was* him…

She looked to her daughter, instantly petrified that he was here to claim her. What would he say? How could she stop him? She couldn't.

It wasn't him, she told herself. It was one of those prophets in a three-piece suit who hand-delivered pamphlets about the world being on the brink of annihilation.

Her world was fine, she reassured herself, still staring at the sprite who comprised the lion's share of all that was important to her.

Lily tipped her head back in an effort to drain water from an empty cup.

The bell rang again.

"Poppy?" her grandmother prompted, glancing her direction. "Will you answer?"

Mentally, Gran was sharp as a tack. Her vision and hearing never failed her. Osteoporosis, however, had impacted her mobility. Her bones were so fragile, Poppy had to be ever vigilant that Lily and her toys weren't underfoot. Her gran would break a hip or worse if she ever stumbled.

There were a lot of things about this living arrangement that made it less than ideal, but both she and Gran were maintaining the status quo, kidding themselves that Gramps was only down at the hardware store and would be back any minute.

"Of course." Poppy snapped out of her stasis and glanced over to be sure the gates on both doorways into the kitchen were closed. All the drawers and cupboards had locks except the one where the plastic dishes were kept. The mixing bowls were a favorite for being dragged out and nested, filled with toys and measuring cups, then dumped without ceremony.

"Keep an eye this way, Gran?" Poppy murmured as she stepped over the gate into the front room, then moved past her seated grandmother to the front door.

Her glance out the side window struck a dark brown bomber jacket over black jeans, but she knew that head, that back with the broad shoulders, that butt and long legs.

His arrival struck like a bus. Like a train that derailed her composure and rattled on for miles, piling one broken thought onto another.

OhGodohGodohGod... *Breathe.* All the way in, all the way out, she reminded herself. But she had always imagined that if this much money showed up on her doorstep, it would be with an oversize check and a television crew. *Not him.*

Rico pivoted from surveying her neighbor's fence and the working grain elevator against the fading Saskatchewan sky. His profile was knife sharp, carved of titanium and godlike.

A hint of shadow was coming in on his jaw, just enough to bend his angelic looks into the fallen kind.

He knocked.

"Poppy—?" her grandmother prompted, tone perplexed by the way she was acting. Or failing to.

How? *How* could he know? Poppy had no doubt that he did. There was absolutely no other reason for this man to be this far off the beaten track. He sure as hell wasn't here to see *her.*

Blood searing with fight or flight, heart pounding, she opened the door.

The full force of his impact slammed through her. The hard angle of his chin, the stern cast of his mouth, his wide shoulders and long legs, and hands held in tense, almost fists.

His jaw hardened as he took her in through mirrored aviators. Their chrome finish was cold and steely. If he'd had a fresh haircut, it had been ruffled by the wind. His boots were alligator, his cologne nothing but crisp, snow-scented air and fuming suspicion.

Poppy lifted her chin and pretended her heart wasn't whirling like a Prairie tornado in her chest.

"Can I help you?" she asked, exactly as she would if he had been a complete stranger.

His hand went to the doorframe. His nostrils twitched as he leaned into the space. "Really?" he asked in a tone of lethal warning.

"Who is it, Poppy?" her grandmother asked.

He stiffened slightly, as though surprised she wasn't alone. Then his mouth curled with disparagement, waiting to see if she would lie.

Poppy swallowed, her entire body buzzing, but she held his gaze through those inscrutable glasses while she said in a strong voice, "Rico, Gran. The man I told you about. From Spain."

There, she silently conveyed. *What do you think of that?*

It wasn't wise to defy him. She knew that by the roil of threat in the pit of her stomach, but she had had to grow up damned fast in the last two years. She was not some naive traveler succumbing to a charmer who turned out to be a thief, or even the starry-eyed maid who had encouraged a philandering playboy to seduce her.

She was a grown woman who had learned how to face her problems head-on.

"Oh?" Gran's tone gave the whole game away in one murmur. There was concern beneath her curiosity. Knowledge. It was less a blithe, *isn't that nice that your friend turned up.* More an alarmed, *Why is he here?*

There was no hiding. None. Poppy might not be able to read this man's eyes, but she read his body language. He wasn't here to ask questions. He was here to confront.

Because he knew she'd had his baby.

Her eyes grew wet with panic, but through her shock, she reacted to seeing her lover, her first and only lover twenty months after they had conceived their daughter. She had thought her brief hour with him a moment of madness. A rush of sex hormones born of dented self-esteem and grand self-delusion.

Since then, her body had been taken over by their daughter. Poppy had been sure her sex drive had dried up and blown away on the Prairie winds. Or at least was firmly in hibernation.

As it turned out, her libido was alive and well. Heat flooded into her with the distant tingles of intimate, erotic memories. Of the cold press of his belt buckle trapped against her thigh, the dampness of perspiration in the hollow of his spine when she ran her hands beneath his open shirt to clutch at him with encouragement. She recalled exactly the way he had kissed the whisker burn on her chin so tenderly, with a growl of apology in his throat. The way he had cupped her breast with restraint, then licked and sucked at her nipple until she was writhing beneath him.

She could feel anew the sharp sensation of him possessing her, so intimate and satisfying, both glorious and ruinous all at once.

She blushed. Hard. Which made the blistering moment feel like hours. She was overflowing at the edges with mortifying awkwardness, searching her mind for something to say, a way to dissemble so he wouldn't know how far he'd thrown her.

"Invite him in, Poppy," her grandmother chided. "You're going to melt the driveway."

She meant because she was letting the heat out, but her words made Poppy blush harder. "Of course," she muttered, flustered. "Come in."

Explanations crowded her tongue as she backed up a step, but stammering them out wouldn't make a difference to a man like him. He might have seemed human and reachable for that stolen hour in his mother's solarium, but she'd realized afterward exactly how ruthless and single-minded he truly was. The passion she'd convinced herself was mutual and startlingly sweet had been a casual, effortless, promptly forgotten seduction on his part.

He'd mended fences with his fiancée the next morning—a woman Poppy knew for a fact he hadn't loved. He'd told Poppy that he'd only agreed to the marriage to gain the presidency of a company and hadn't seemed distressed in the least that the wedding had been called off.

Embarrassment at being such an easy conquest had her staring at his feet as she closed the door behind him. "Will you take off your boots, please?"

Her request gave him pause. In his mother's house, everyone wore shoes, especially guests. A single pair of their usual footwear cost more than Poppy had made in her four months of working in that house.

Rico toed off his boots and set them against the wall. Then he tucked his sunglasses into his chest pocket. His eyes were slate-gray with no spark of blue or flecks of hot green that had surrounded his huge pupils that day in the solarium.

After setting his cold, granite gaze against her until she was chilled through, he glanced past her, into the front room of the tiny bungalow her grandfather had built for his wife while working as a linesman for the hydro company. It was the home where Gramps had brought his bride the day they married. It was where they had brought home their only son and where they had raised their only grandchild.

Seeing him in it made Poppy both humble and defensive. It didn't compare to the grandiose villa he'd been raised in, but it was her home. Poppy wasn't ashamed of it, only struck by how he could so easily jeopardize all of this with a snap of his fingers. This house wasn't even hers. If he had come here to claim Lily, she had very few resources at her disposal. Maybe it would even be held against her that she didn't have much and he could offer so much more.

"Hello," he greeted her grandmother as she muted the television and set the remote aside.

"This is Rico Montero, Gran. My grandmother, Eleanor Harris."

"*The* Rico?"

"Yes."

Rico's brows went up a fraction, making Poppy squirm.

"It's nice to meet you. Finally." Gran started to rise.

Poppy stepped forward to help her, but Rico was quick to touch her grandmother's arm and say, "Please. There's no need to stand. It's a pleasure to meet you."

Oh, he knew how to use the warmth of his accented voice to slay a woman, young or old. Poppy almost fell for it herself, thinking he sounded reassuring when he was actually here to destroy their small, simple world.

Yet she had to go through the motions of civility. Pretend he was simply a guest who had dropped by.

Gran smiled up at him with glimmers of adoration. "I was getting up to give you privacy to talk. I imagine you'll want that."

"In that case, yes please. Allow me to help you." Rico moved to her side and supported her with gentle care.

Don't leave me alone with him, Poppy wanted to cry, but she slid Gran's walker in front of her. "Thank you, Gran."

"I'll listen to the radio in my room until you come for me." Her grandmother nodded and shuffled her way into the hall. "Remember the biscuits."

The biscuits. The least of her worries. Poppy couldn't smell them yet, but the timer would go off any second. She moved her body into the path toward the kitchen door, driven by mother-bear instincts.

"Why are you here?" Her voice quavered with the volume of emotions rocketing through her—shock and protectiveness and fear. Culpability and anger and other deeper yearnings she didn't want to acknowledge.

"I want to see her." He set his shoulders in a way that told her he wasn't going anywhere until he did.

Behind her, the sound of bowls coming out of the cupboard and being knocked around re-assured her that Lily was perfectly fine without eyes on her.

A suffocating feeling sat on her chest and kept a vise around her throat. She wanted him to answer the rest of her question. What was he going to do about this discovery? She wasn't ready to face the answer.

Playing for time, she strangled out, "How did you find out?"

If they hadn't been standing so close, she might have missed the way his pupils dilated and his breath seemed to catch as though taking a blow. In the next second, the impression of shock was gone. A fierce, angry light of satisfaction gleamed in his eyes.

"Sorcha saw a photo you posted of a baby who looks like Mateo. I investigated."

Odd details from the last two weeks fell into place. She dropped her chin in outrage. "That new dad at the day care! I thought he was hitting on me, asking all those questions."

Rico's dark brows slammed together. "He came on to you?"

"He said he took Lily's cup by mistake, but it was an excuse to talk to me." Poppy was obviously still batting a thousand where her poor judgement of men was concerned.

"He took it for a DNA sample."

"That is just plain *wrong*," she said indignantly.

"I agree that I shouldn't have to resort to

such measures to learn I have a child. *Why didn't you tell me?*" he asked through clenched teeth.

He had some right to the anger he poured over ice. She acknowledged that. But she wasn't a villain. Just a stupid girl who'd gotten herself in trouble by the wrong man and had made the best of a difficult situation.

"I didn't realize I was pregnant until you were married. By then, it was all over the gossip sites that Faustina was also expecting."

It shouldn't have been such a blow when she'd read that. His wedding had been called off for a *day*. Loads of people had a moment of cold feet before they went through with the ceremony. She accepted she was collateral damage to that.

She had been feeling very down on herself by then, though. She ought to have known better than to let herself get carried away. She hadn't taken any precautions. She had been careless and foolish, believing him when he had told her that he and his fiancée hadn't been sleeping together.

The whole thing had made her feel so humiliatingly stupid. She had hoped never to have to face him or her gullibility ever again.

So much for that.

And facing him was so *hard. He* was so hard. A muscle was pulsing in his jaw, but the rest of him was like concrete. Pitiless and unmoved.

"Faustina died a year ago last September," he said in that gritty tone. "You've had ample opportunity to come forward."

As she recalled the terrible headlines she'd read with morbid anguish, her heart turned inside out with agony for him. She had nursed thoughts every day of telling him he had a child after all, but…

"I'm sorry for your loss." She truly was. No matter what he'd felt for his wife, losing his child must have been devastating.

His expression stiffened and he recoiled slightly at her words of condolence.

"My grandfather was quite ill," she continued huskily. "If you recall, that's why I came home. He passed just before Christmas. Gran needed me. There hasn't been a right time to shake things up."

His expression altered slightly as he absorbed that.

She imagined his sorrow to be so much more acute than hers. She mourned a man who had lived a full life and who had passed without pain or regret. They'd held a service that had been a true celebration of his long life.

While Rico's baby had been cheated of even starting its own.

Rico nodded acceptance of her excuse with only a pained flicker as acknowledgment of what must have been his very personal and intensely painful loss.

Had grief driven him here? Was he trying to replace his lost child with his living one? *No.* The thought of it agonized her. Lily wasn't some placeholder for another child. It cracked her heart in half that he might think she could be.

Before she could find words to address that fear, the timer beeped in the kitchen.

Lily had become very quiet, too, which was a sure sign of trouble. Poppy turned to glance around the doorframe. Lily sat with one finger poking at the tiny hole on a bowl's rim, where the bowl was meant to be hung on a nail.

Firm hands settled on her shoulders. Rico's untamed scent and the heat of his body surrounded her. He looked past her into the kitchen. At his daughter.

Poppy told herself not to look, but she couldn't help it. She was afraid he would be resentful that Lily had lived when his other baby hadn't. Even as she feared he was planning to steal her, she perversely would be more agonized if he rejected her. He had come all this way. That meant he felt something toward her, didn't it? On some level, he wanted her?

His expression was unreadable, face so closed and tense, her heart dropped into her shoes.

Love her, she wanted to beg. *Please.*

His breath sucked in with an audible hiss.

He took in so much air, his chest swelled to brush against her back. His hands tightened on her shoulders.

At the subtle noise, Lily lifted her gorgeous gray eyes, so like her father's. A huge smile broke across her face.

"Mama." The bowls were forgotten and she crawled toward them, pulling herself up on the gate.

Lily's smile propelled Poppy through all her hard days. She was Poppy's world. Poppy's parents were distant, her grandfather gone, her grandmother... Well, Poppy didn't want to think about losing her even though she knew it was inevitable.

But she had this wee girl and she was everything.

"Hello, button." Poppy scooped up her daughter and kissed her cheek, never able to resist that soft, plump bite of sweet-smelling warmth. Then she brushed at Lily's hands because it didn't matter how many times she swept or vacuumed, Lily found the specks and dust bunnies in her eager exploration of her world.

This time when Poppy looked to Rico, she saw his reaction more clearly. He was trying to mask it with stoicism, but the intensity in his gaze ate up Lily's snowy skin and cupid's-bow mouth.

Her emotions seesawed again. She had needed this. Her heart had needed to see him accept his daughter, but he was a threat, too.

"This is Lily." Her name was tellingly senti-mental, not the sort of romantic notion Poppy should have given in to, but since her own name was a flower, it had seemed right.

Poppy faltered, not ready to tell Lily this was Daddy.

Lily brought her fingers to her mouth and said, "Ee."

"Eat?" Poppy asked and slid her hand down from her throat. "You're hungry?"

Lily nodded.

"Sign language?" Rico asked, voice sharp-ening with concern. "Is she hearing im-paired?"

"It's sign language for babies. They teach it at day care. She's trying to say words, but this works for now." Poppy stepped over the gate into the kitchen and snapped off the oven. "Do you, um…" She couldn't believe this was happening, but she wanted to put off the hard conversations as long as possible. "Will you join us for dinner?"

A brief pause, then, "You don't have to cook. I can order something in."

"From where?" Poppy chuckled dryly as she set Lily in her chair. "We have Chinese take-out and a pizza palace." *Not* his usual standard. "The soup is already made."

She tied on Lily's bib and set the bowl of cooled soup and a small flat spoon in front of her.

Lily grabbed the spoon and batted it into the thick soup.

"Renting the car was a challenge for my staff," he mentioned absently, frowning as Lily missed her mouth and smeared soup across her own cheek.

"Gran said you're driving something fancy,"

Poppy recalled. She had forgotten to look, unable to see past the man to anything else.

"An Alfa Romeo, but it's a sedan."

With a car seat? Poppy almost bobbled the sheet of biscuits as she took them from the oven. "Are you, um, staying at the motel?"

He snorted. "No. My staff have taken a cottage an hour from here so I have a bed if I decide to stay."

Poppy tried to read his expression, but he was watching Lily, frowning with exasperation as Lily turned her head, open mouth looking for the end of the spoon.

In a decisive move, he removed his jacket and draped it over the back of a chair. Then he picked up the teaspoon beside Poppy's setting and turned the chair to face Lily. He sat and began helping her eat.

Poppy caught her breath, arrested by the sight of this dynamic man feeding their daughter. His strapping muscles strained the seams in his shirt, telling of his tension, but he calmly waited for Lily to try before he gently touched the tip of his teaspoon to her bottom lip. He let Lily lean into eating it before they both went after the next spoonful in the bowl.

Had she dreamed of this? *Was* she dreaming? It was such a sweet sight her ovaries locked fresh eggs into their chambers, preparing to launch and create another Lily or five. All she needed was one glance from him that contained something other than accusation or animosity.

"You said the timing was wrong."

It took her a moment to realize he was harking back to the day they'd conceived her. She could only stand there in chagrined silence while a coal of uncomfortable heat burned in her middle, spreading a blush upward, into her throat and cheeks and ending in a pressure behind her eyes.

He glanced at her. "When we—"

"I know what you mean," she cut him off, turning away to stack hot biscuits onto a plate, suffused in virginal discomfiture all over again. He'd noticed blood and asked if she had started her cycle. She'd been too embarrassed to tell him it was her first time. She was too embarrassed to say it now.

"I should have taken something after." She didn't tell him she had hung around in Spain an extra day, hoping he would come find her only to hear the wedding was back on.

That news had propelled her from the scene, consuming her with thoughts of what a pushover she'd been for a man on a brief furlough from his engagement. Contraception should have been top of mind, but…

"I was traveling, trying to make my flight." Poppy hugged herself, trying to keep the fissure in her chest from widening. She felt *so* exposed right now and couldn't meet his penetrating stare. "I honestly did think the timing was wrong. I didn't even realize I was pregnant until I was starting to show. I had next to no symptoms." There'd even been a bit of spotting. "I thought the few signs I did have were stress related. Gramps's health was deteriorating. By the time it was confirmed, you were married." She finally looked at him and let one hand come out, palm up, beseeching for understanding.

There was no softening in his starkly unforgiving expression.

"I didn't think you would—" She couldn't say aloud that she had worried he wouldn't want his daughter. Not when he was feeding Lily with such care.

Helpless tears pressed behind her eyes.

He knew what she had almost said and sent her another flat stare of muted fury. "I want her, Poppy. That's why I'm here."

Her heart swerved in her chest. The pressure behind her eyes increased.

"Don't look so terrified." He returned his attention to Lily, who was waiting with an open mouth like a baby bird. "I'm not here to kidnap her."

"What, then?" She clung tight to her elbows, needing something to anchor her. Needing to know what was going to happen.

"Am I supposed to ignore her?"

"No." His question poked agonizing pins into the most sensitive spots on her soul.

"But I was afraid you might," she admitted. "I thought it would be easier on both of us if you didn't know, rather than if you did, but didn't care."

Another wall-of-concrete stare, then a clearly pronounced, "I care." He scraped the spoon through the thick soup. "And not only because the maids in my mother's house are bound to recognize the resemblance the way Sorcha's nanny did and begin to talk. She's a Montero. She's entitled to the benefits that brings."

Now he stood directly on Poppy's pride.

"We don't *need* help, Rico. That's another reason I never told you. I didn't want you to think I was looking for a handout. We're fine."

"The day care with the nonexistent security is 'fine'? What happens when it's known her father is wealthy? We take basic precautions, Poppy. You don't even have an alarm system. I didn't hear you click a lock when you opened the front door."

They lived in rural Canada. People worried about squirrels in the attic, not burglars in the bedroom.

"No one knows you're rich. Gran is the only person who even knows your name and I wasn't entirely forthcoming about…who you really are." Poppy gave a tendril of hair a distracted brush so it tucked behind her ear for all of five seconds. "Do you mind if I get her? She takes medication on a schedule and needs to eat beforehand. We try to stick to a routine."

"Of course." He lifted two fingers off the bowl he still held steady for Lily's jabs of her own spoon. "We'll discuss how we'll proceed after Lily is in bed."

CHAPTER TWO

POPPY OPENED THE GATE and set it aside, leaving Rico to continue feeding his daughter.

He had watched Sorcha and Cesar do this countless times with their sons. He'd always thought it a messy process best left to nannies, but discovered it was oddly satisfying. His older nephew, Enrique, had reached an age where he held conversations—some that were inadvertently amusing—but babies had always struck Rico as something that required a lot of intensive care without offering much in return.

Sorcha had pressed her sons onto him over the years, which had achieved her goal of provoking feelings of affection in him, but, like his parents, he viewed children as something between a duty and a social experiment. Even when he had briefly believed Faustina had been carrying his heir, the idea of being a father had only been that—an idea. Not a concept he had fully internalized or a role he understood how to fulfill effectively. Fatherhood hadn't been something he had viewed with anticipation the way other creative projects had inspired him.

But here he sat, watching eyes the same color as his own track to the doorway where Poppy had disappeared. A wet finger pointed. "Mama."

"She'll be right back." He imagined Poppy would actually spend a few minutes talking to her grandmother in private.

Lily smiled before she leaned forward, mouth open.

Damn, she was beautiful. It wasn't bias, either. Or his fondness for the nephews she resembled. She had her mother's fresh snowy skin and red-gold lashes, healthy round cheeks and a chin that suggested she had his stubbornness along with his eyes.

A ridiculous swell of pride went through him even as he reminded himself that he didn't know conclusively that she was his. The DNA test off the cup had been a long shot and hadn't proved paternity either way.

Nevertheless, he'd been propelled as much by the absence of truth as he would have been by the presence of it. From the time Sorcha had revealed her suspicion, a ferocious fire had begun to burn in him, one stoked by yet another female keeping secrets from him. Huge, life-altering secrets.

He hadn't wanted to wait for more tests, or hire lawyers, or even pick up the phone and *ask*. He had needed to see for himself.

Who? a voice asked in the back of his head.

Both, he acknowledged darkly. He had needed to set eyes on the baby, whom he recognized on a deeply biological level, and on the woman who haunted his memories.

Poppy had seemed so guileless. So refreshingly honest and real.

He thought back to that day, searching for the moment where he'd been tricked into making a baby with a woman who had then kept her pregnancy a secret.

He remembered thinking his mother wouldn't appreciate him popping a bottle of the wedding champagne—even though she'd procured a hundred cases that had been superfluous because the wedding had been called off.

Rico had helped himself to his father's scotch in the billiards room instead. He had taken it through to the solarium, planning to bum a cigarette from the gardener. It was a weakness he had kicked years ago, but the craving still hit sometimes, when his life went sideways.

It was the end of the day, though. The sun-warmed room was packed to the gills with lilies brought in to replace the ones damaged by a late frost. The solarium was deserted and the worktable in the back held a dirty ashtray and a cigarette pack that was empty.

"Oh! I'm so sorry."

The woman spoke in English, sounding American, maybe. He turned to see the red-headed maid who'd been on the stairs an hour earlier, when Faustina had been throwing a tantrum that had included one of his mother's Wedgwoods, punctuating the end of their engagement. He would come to understand much later what sort of pressure Faustina had been under, but at the time, she'd been an unreasonable, clichéd diva of a bride by whom he'd been relieved to have been jilted.

And the interruption by the fresh-faced maid had been a welcome distraction.

Her name was Poppy. He knew that without looking at the embroidered tag on her uniform. She stared with wide doe eyes, the proverbial deer in headlights, startled to come upon him pilfering smokes as though he was thirteen again.

"I mean…um…*perdón.*" She pivoted to go back the way she'd come.

"Wait. Do you have a cigarette?" he asked in English.

"Me? No." She swung back around. "Do I look like a smoker?"

Her horror at resembling such a thing amused him.

"Do I?" he drawled. "What do we look like? The patriarchy?"

"I don't know." She chuckled and blushed slightly, her clear skin glowing pink beneath the gold of filtered sunlight, like late afternoon on untouched ski slopes. "I, um, didn't know you smoked." She swallowed and linked her hands shyly before her.

Ah. She'd been watching him, too, had she?

His mother's staff had been off-limits since his brother's first kiss with a maid before Rico had even had a shot at one. He didn't usually notice one from another, but Poppy had snagged his attention with her vibrant red hair. Curls were springing free of the bundle she'd scraped it into, teasing him with fantasies of releasing the rest and digging his hands into the kinky mass.

The rest of her was cute as hell, too, if a bit skinny and young. Maybe it was her lack of makeup. That mouth, unpainted, but with a plump bottom lip and a playful top was all woman. Her brows were so light, they were almost blond, her chin pert, her eyes a gentle yet very direct dark ale-brown.

No, he reminded himself. He was engaged.

Actually, he absorbed with a profound sense of liberation, he wasn't. Faustina had firmly and unequivocally ended their engagement, despite his mother's best efforts to talk her back on board.

His mother had retired with a wet compress and a migraine tablet. He had come in here because he couldn't go home. His house was being renovated for the bride who was now refusing to share her life with him. Driving all the way to his brother's house to get blind drunk had felt like an unnecessary delay.

"I don't smoke." He dropped the empty pack and picked up his drink. "I rebelled for a year or so when I was a teen, but it seemed like a good excuse to talk with Ernesto about football and other inconsequential topics." He was sick to death of jabbering about weddings and duty and the expected impact on the family fortune.

Her shoulders softened and her red-gold

brows angled with sympathy. "I'm really sorry." She sounded adorably sincere. "I'll, um, give you privacy to…"

"Wallow in heartbreak? Unnecessary." Faustina's outburst had been the sum total of passion their marriage was likely to have borne. "I don't want to chase you away if you're on your break."

"No, I'm done. I know we're not supposed to cut through here to get to the change rooms over the garage, but I was hoping to catch Ernesto myself. He gives me a lift sometimes."

"Are you American?" he asked.

Her strawberry blond lashes flickered in surprise, her expression growing shy. Aware.

An answering awareness teased through him, waking the wolf inside him. That starved beast had been locked inside a cave the last six months, but unexpectedly found himself free of the heavy chain he'd placed around his own neck. The sun was in his eyes, the wind was ruffling his fur and he was picking up the scent of a willing female. He was itching to romp and tumble and mate.

"Canada." She cleared her throat. "Saskatchewan. A little town with nothing but canola fields and clouds." She shook her head. "You wouldn't have heard of it."

"How did you wind up here?"

"I'd tell you, but I'd bore you to death." Despite her words, a pretty smile played around her mouth and a soft blush of pleasure glowed under her skin.

"I came out here to smoke. Clearly I have a death wish."

After a small chuckle, she cautioned, "Okay, but stop me if you feel light-headed."

Definitely not bored, he thought with a private smile. She wasn't merely a first cigarette years after quitting, either. To be sure he was drawing in this lighthearted flirting with avid greed, but he found himself enjoying her wit. He was genuinely intrigued by her.

"I saved up to trek around Europe with a friend, but she broke her ankle on the second day and flew home." She folded her arms, protective or defensive, maybe. "I tagged along with some students from a hostel coming here, but a few days after we arrived, one of them stole everything I had." She slapped a what-can-you-do? smile on it, but the tension around her eyes and mouth told him she was still upset.

He frowned. "Did you go to the police?"

"It was my fault." She flinched with self-recrimination. "I gave him my card to get some cash for me one morning. He must have made a copy or something. Three days later he'd syphoned all of my savings and was gone. I had my passport, a bag of raisins and my hairbrush. Losing my camera gutted me the most. It was a gift and my memory card was still in it, not that I'd had the chance to fill it. It was a huge bummer." She summed up with philosophical lightness.

"You're a photographer?"

"Not anymore," she asserted with disgust, then shrugged it off. "At least I had prepaid for a week at the hostel. I asked around and got on with a temp agency. I was brought in to help clean the pool house and guest cottage. Darna liked my work and asked me to stay on full-time in the big house. I've been saving for a ticket home ever since."

"How much do you need?" He reached into his pocket.

"Oh, no!" She halted him, horrified. "I have enough. I just worked it out with Darna that today was my last day. She thought she would need me through the rest of June for—" She halted, wincing as she realized who she was talking to.

Rico let the awkwardness hang in the air, not to punish, but because he was finding her candor so refreshing.

"It seemed like the wedding was going to be really beautiful." She sounded apologetic. "I'm sorry it didn't work out."

He wasn't. That was the naked truth, but he deflected by saying, "I've heard that Canadians apologize a lot. I didn't believe it."

"We do. Sorry." She winked on that one.

Was she sorry?

Rico came back to the tap of a dirty spoon against the back of his knuckles.

Poppy had been twenty-two, disillusioned

after being shortchanged on chasing her dreams, yet willing to come home to fulfill family obligations. He had understood that pressure and had confided his own reasons for going along with family expectations.

That affinity had led to a kiss and his feet had somehow carried her to the sheet-draped furniture hidden amongst the jungle of fragrant lilies.

Since learning about Lily, he'd been convinced Poppy had somehow tricked him the way Faustina had, for her own nefarious ends.

That suspicion wasn't playing as strongly now that he was here. Her home was unpretentious, dated and showing signs of age, but neat and well cared for. Her bond with her grandmother and daughter seemed genuine and from the reports he'd commissioned, she was this side of financially solvent. She didn't even have a speeding ticket on her record.

He'd picked up two on his way here, but that was beside the point.

In the past, he had seen what he wanted to

see. He couldn't allow himself to be so credulous again.

He made himself take a cool moment to watch Lily's concentrated effort to touch the end of her spoon into the soup and bring the taste to her mouth. She grinned as she succeeded, spoon caught between her tiny white teeth.

He had no proof, but he was convinced she was his. He *had* to claim her.

As for Poppy, he was still absorbing the impact she continued to have on him. He still reacted physically to her. One look at her in jeans and a loose pullover and his mouth had started to water. No makeup, hair gathered into a messy knot of kinks on her head, wariness like a halo around her, yet he'd had to restrain himself from reaching for her. Not to grab or take possession, but simply to *touch*. Fill his hands with the textures of her.

Was her skin as smooth and soft as his erotic dreams replayed? Would her nipples tighten if he licked then blew lightly again? Did her voice still break in orgasm and would that sound once again send pleasurable shivers down his back?

That chemistry was a weakness, one that warned him to keep his guard up, but it didn't deter him from his plan one iota.

In fact, it stoked a fire of anticipation deep in the pit of his belly.

Poppy's tension remained through dinner, even though Rico went on a charm offensive against her grandmother, breaking out levels even Poppy hadn't realized he possessed, asking after her health and offering condolences over Gramps.

"I'm very sorry to hear you lost him. I remember Poppy saying he wasn't well, just before she left Spain."

Poppy released a subtle snort, suspecting he only recalled that detail because she had reminded him of it an hour ago.

He frowned with affront. "I asked you why you weren't using the money you'd saved to see more of Europe. You said your grandparents needed help moving into a care facility."

For one second, she saw glints of blue and green in his irises, telling her he remembered *everything* about that day.

A spike of tingling heat drove sharp as a lance through her. She crossed her legs, bumping her foot against his shin in the process and sending a reverberation of deeper awareness through her whole body.

"We were talking about moving," Gran said, forcing Rico to break their eye contact. "I couldn't look after Bill myself, but having Poppy here bought us an extra year in our home." Gran squeezed her hand over Poppy's, the strength in her grip heart-wrenchingly faint. "He would have faded all the faster if we'd been forced to leave this house. I'll always be grateful to her for giving us that. I don't know what I would have done if she hadn't been here in the months since he's been gone, either. She's been our special blessing her whole life."

"Gran." Poppy teared up. She knew darned well she'd been more of a burden.

"And Lily is ever so precious, too." Gran smiled at the baby. "But it's time."

"Time?" Poppy repeated with muted alarm.

"I'll call your aunt Sheila in the morning," she said of her sister, patting Poppy's hand before she removed her touch. "I'm on the top of the list at that facility near her apartment. I'm sure I can stay with her until a room opens up."

"Gran, *no*."

"Poppy. We both know I shouldn't have been here this winter, making more work for you on top of looking after the baby. You were shoveling the drive on your one day off to get me to the doctor's office. I have no business near that ice by the front steps, either. You're penning up Lily, worrying I'll trip over her. *I'm* worried. No, I don't want to hold you back from the life you ought to be leading."

"This *is* the life I want to lead." Poppy's chin began to crinkle the way Lily's did when she was coming down with a cold and Poppy had to leave her at day care.

"Oh, is your fancy man moving in with us, then?" Gran asked.

"I see where Poppy gets her spark." A faint smile touched Rico's lips. "Poppy and I have details to work out, but you're right that my life is in Spain. I'm here to marry her and take Poppy and Lily home with me."

After a brief, illogical spike of elation, Poppy's heart fell with that bombshell news. Her mind exploded. He wasn't wrenching their daughter from her arms, but she wasn't relieved in the least. She immediately knew this wasn't about her. He'd married for coldly practical reasons the first time. He might dazzle her grandmother with kindness and charisma, but it was a dispassionate move to get what he wanted by the quickest, most efficient means. She shouldn't be shocked at all by his goal or his methods.

"*My* life is here with Gran," Poppy insisted shakily. "She needs me nearby, even if she moves into assisted care."

"Poppy." The fragility of her grandmother's hand draped over hers again. "What I need is to know that when I'm gone, you're set-tled with someone who will take care of you and Lily. That person ought to be her father." She patted lightly, saying with quiet power, "I know what this would have meant to you."

If her own father had shown up to take her home, Gran meant. The hot pressure behind her eyes increased.

Even so, there was a part of Poppy that simply heard it as her grandmother wishing Poppy would cease to be a burden upon her.

A spiked ball lodged behind Poppy's breast-bone, one she couldn't swallow away. It was so sharp it made tears sting her eyes.

"It's obvious Poppy won't be comfortable unless you're comfortable, Eleanor. Give us a chance to finish our talk. Then you and I will discuss your options. I'm sure we can find solutions that satisfy all of us."

Poppy wanted to shout a giant, scoffing, *Ha!* She rose to clear the table.

CHAPTER THREE

POPPY BATHED LILY and put her to bed, not giving her daughter the attention she deserved because her mind was still whirling with Rico showing up and demanding more than his daughter. *Marriage.*

Had she spun that fantasy in her girlish mind? Yes. Even before she slept with him. She had been fascinated by him for weeks, acutely aware of him whether he was making a dry comment or sipping a glass of orange juice. He'd seemed aloof, but in a laid-back way. When she had overheard Faustina going full Bridezilla, shattering a vase and screaming that their wedding was off, Rico had only said in a calm voice, "Let me have the bottom of that. I'll have to replace it."

Deep down, she'd been thrilled that Faustina had ended things. Happy for him.

In the solarium, he'd been that charming man she'd seen tonight at dinner, the one who expressed so much interest in others, it was easy to miss that he gave away very little about himself.

He had told her enough that day, however. Enough that she had been fooled into thinking he liked her. That there was a spark of... *something.*

She'd been wrong. This was the real man. He was severe and intimidating, not raising his voice because he didn't have to. His wishes, delivered in that implacable tone, were sheer power. She instinctively knew there was no shifting him on the course he had decided.

He didn't want her, though. She was merely an obstacle he was overcoming as expediently as possible. Her grandmother would see this marriage as a move toward security, but Poppy refused to trust his offer so easily. What if he got her over there and promptly divorced her? Took her to court for custody?

There was no way she could survive without Lily.

Lily settled and Poppy went to the front room. Rico had finished the calls he'd been making and was chatting with her grandmother.

Having him in her home made her squirm. It was her private space where she revealed her true self in faded, toothless photos on the wall next to some of her earliest photography efforts. She and Gran had been working their way through a box of paperback romances that Poppy had picked up at a garage sale and Poppy's latest passionate cover was splayed open on the coffee table.

On the mantel stood Poppy's framed employee of the month certificate. Her boss at the bus depot had given it to her as a joke. Aside from him, she was the only employee and she was part-time. Gran had had her first good laugh in ages when Poppy had brought it home. Then they'd wept because Gramps would have enjoyed it, too.

Beside the certificate stood a generic birthday card from last month signed, *Love, Mom*. It was the only message besides the preprinted poem.

Rico was seeing far too much of *her* in this space. Maybe gathering ammunition for why his daughter couldn't stay here. A man so low on sentiment wouldn't recognize the comfort in the worn furniture and the value of memory-infused walls.

"The weatherman said it's a good night for stargazing," Gran was telling Rico while nodding at the television. "You might even see the northern lights."

"It's freezing outside," Poppy protested. "Literally." Spring might be a few days away on the calendar, but there was still thick frost on her windshield every morning.

"Bundle up." Gran dismissed Poppy's argument with the hardy practicality of a woman who'd lived on the prairies her whole life. "Your grandfather and I always came to agreement walking around Fisher's Pond. I have the phone right here." She touched the table where the cordless phone lived. "I'll call if Lily wakes and fusses."

Poppy glanced at Rico, hoping he would say it was late and he would come back tomorrow.

"I left my gloves in the car. I'll collect them on my way."

She bit back a huff and layered up, pulling on boots, mittens and a toque before tramping into what was actually a fairly mild night, considering the sky was clear and there was still snow on the ground.

The moon turned the world a bluish daylight and her footsteps crunched after Rico as they started away from the car. He wound a red scarf around his neck as they walked.

"Before today, I had only flown over prairies, never driven through them." His breath clouded as he spoke.

"Were you fighting to stay awake?"

"No, but it's very relaxing. Gives you time and space to think."

She didn't ask him what he'd been thinking about, just took him past the last house on their street, then along the path in the snow toward the depression that was Fisher's Pond.

It was a busy place midwinter. Neighborhood children played hockey every chance they got, but signs were posted now that the ice was thinning and no longer safe. The makeshift benches and lights were gone leaving only the trampled ring around the pond that was popular with dog walkers in summer. Tonight, they had the place to themselves.

"I haven't seen the Milky Way like that, either," he said, nodding at the seam of stars ripped open across the sky. "Not clear and massive like that."

"Rico, I can't go to Spain with you."

"I can hire a live-in care aid." His tone became very businesslike. "Or support her in any facility she chooses. You can be back here within a day if concerns arise. Do not use your grandmother as an excuse to keep my daughter from me."

Wow. She rubbed her mitten against her cold nose, trying to keep the tip of it from growing numb.

"She's not an excuse. She's my family."

He absorbed that, then asked, "Where are your parents? Why has it fallen on you to look after your grandparents?"

"I wanted to." She hugged herself. "They've always been good to me. Even when I came home pregnant."

Especially then. Buying the assisted-living unit would have required selling the house, leaving Poppy without anywhere to live. It had been everyone's wish that they stay together in that house while Gramps was so sick, but Gran was right. They couldn't sustain this. Poppy had been mentally preparing herself for spending the summer clearing out the house. That didn't mean she was ready to move with her daughter around the globe, though.

"Did your parents pass away? Have you always lived with them?"

"I have, but my parents are alive. Divorced. Dad works in the oil patch." She tried not to sound as forlorn as she had always felt when talking about her parents. "He shows up every few months for a week or so, sleeps on the couch and does some repairs. He used to give Gran money sometimes, for taking care of me. I think he gambles most of what he makes. It's one of those things no one in the family talks about, but money has always been an issue with him."

"Thus the divorce?"

"I'm sure that was part of it. Mom had her own issues." She turned from the cleared patch that faced the pond and started on the path around it.

She hated that she had to reveal her deepest shame, but he ought to know it, so he would understand her reasons for refusing to marry him.

"They were really young when they had me. Mom was only nineteen. Not ready for the responsibility of being a parent. My dad brought her here to live with his parents then left to work far away. Mom stuck around until I was two, then she started moving around, living the life she thought she was entitled to, I guess."

"Partying? Drugs?"

"Freedom, mostly." Poppy understood now how overwhelming parenting was, but *she* hadn't dropped her daughter like a hot potato just because it was hard. "She didn't want to be a mom. She wanted to 'explore her potential.'" Poppy air-quoted the phrase. "She tried modeling in Toronto and worked as a flight attendant out of Montreal. She was a music promoter in Halifax, went to Vancouver to work on a cruise ship. Followed a man to India for a year then came back and opened a yoga studio in California. That's how she met her current husband, teaching one of his ex-wives to downward dog. He's a movie producer. They have two kids."

Two sulky, spoiled children who complained about the meals Poppy's mother cooked for them and the music lessons and soccer practices she drove them to.

Poppy tried not to hate them. They were family, but they were also entitled little brats.

"You never lived with her?" Rico asked behind her.

"By the time she was settled, I was starting high school. Bringing me across the border even for a visit was more bureaucracy than she wanted to face. She still hasn't seen Lily except over the tablet. I think she wishes I had never been born. Not in a spiteful way, but she would rather pretend her youthful mistake had never happened."

The path became streaked by the shadows of a copse of trees. She plodded into it, trying not to be depressed by her parents' neglect when they'd left her with such amazing grandparents.

"What I'm hearing is that you wish both of your parents had taken steps to bring you to live with them."

"Is that what you're hearing?" She stopped and turned, thinking her grandparents had been onto something because there was safety in the darkness, where her vulnerability wasn't painted in neon letters across her face. "Because I've come to realize they did me a favor, leaving me with people who tucked me in and told me they loved me every night."

She had surprised him by turning to confront him. He had pulled up, but stood really close. His face was striped by ivory and cobalt.

"Have you told them? Your parents?" she asked.

"I told them she was likely mine, even though the DNA results were inconclusive. I said—"

"What?" Poppy's elbows went stiff as she punched the air by her thighs. "Why did you even *come* here if you didn't *know*?"

"Because I had to know," he said tightly, "Your guilty expression when you opened the door was all the proof I needed."

She was such a dope, confirming his suspicions before he even *knew*. How did he disarm her so easily again and again?

"What was their reaction?" she asked, focusing on her deeper concerns. The *duque* and *duquesa* had struck Poppy as being aliens in human skin, assimilating on earth well enough not to be detected, but incapable of relating to normal people or showing genuine emotion.

"They asked to be kept informed."

"I see. And is your mother still on the hunt for the next Señora Montero?"

"How the hell do you know that?"

"I'm capable of reading a headline."

"Elevate your browsing choices. Gossip sites are garbage. If you wanted to know what I was doing with my life, you should have called *me*."

"I'm more interested in how your mother is going to react to Lily."

"She'll accept a fait accompli. She's done it before."

When Cesar's indiscretion with Sorcha had resulted in Enrique. But as far as Poppy could tell, Rico's father had barely noticed he had a grandson while his mother had given Enrique tight smiles and offered unsolicited suggestions on how he could be improved. *He looks due for a haircut, Sorcha.*

So Poppy snorted her disbelief. "I've seen

what her type of 'acceptance' looks like and it's colder than an arctic vortex."

"Be careful, Poppy."

"That wasn't a cheap shot. I'm saying Lily is far too important to me to set her up to be the subject of criticism and disapproval for the rest of her life. If they're going to treat her like a stain on the family name, I won't take her anywhere near them."

He probably thought she should be grateful he was planning to let her accompany him and her daughter, but he only said, "They're not demonstrative people. There will be no welcome embrace from either of them. Reconcile yourself to that right now. They do, however, bring other strengths to the table. We Monteros look after our own."

"My stepfather can put her in movies if she decides she wants wealth and fame."

"Wealth is not fortune, fame is not standing," he stated pithily. "What sort of future are you planning for her? You'll date, perhaps introduce her to a few contenders and, one day, when you're convinced you're in love, you'll allow another man to raise *my* child without any of the genuine advantages to which she's entitled? In ignorance of her family and the attached opportunities overseas? No. I won't let you deny her what's rightfully hers."

"It's not up to you. And don't say it like that! 'When I'm *convinced* I'm in love.' *I love Lily.* Try to tell me that feeling is a figment of my imagination." She would knock him through the ice. "Do *you* plan to love her? Because, given what I saw of your upbringing, you were never shown how."

A profound silence crashed over them.

"Just as you were never taught to hold your temper in favor of a civil conversation?" Oh, he sounded lethal. The cold in the air began to penetrate her clothes.

"Answer the question," she insisted. "My love for Lily took root the day I learned I was pregnant." It had grown so expansive her body couldn't contain the force of it. It quivered in her voice as she continued. "I won't set her up to yearn for something from you that will never happen. I've been there and it is far too painful a thing to wish onto my child. *You know it is.*"

She had pushed herself right out onto the ledge of getting way too personal. She knew she had, but that was how much her daughter meant to her.

The umbrage radiating off him should have flash-melted the snow and razed the trees, illuminating the skies in an explosion of light.

Even so, she nudged even further by warning through her teeth, "Don't shove your way into her life unless you intend to be there every single moment, in every possible way she might need you to be."

His hands jammed into his pockets and his profile was slashed with shadows.

"You—" Something made him bite off whatever he had been about to say. He made a sucking noise through clenched teeth, as though enduring the removal of a bullet or something equally wounding. "My brother's sons are not unhappy. He had my same upbringing. He's managed to become quite attached. I would expect to form that sort of connection with my own child."

She was glad for the dark then, because sudden, pitying tears froze to her lashes. His words were such a careful admission that he was fine with not being loved as a child, but would find a way to extend his heart to his daughter.

For that reason alone, for the opportunity to gift him with his child's unconditional love, she knew she would have to allow him into Lily's life.

"Even so…" She folded her arms and squished handfuls of her quilted sleeves with her woolen mittens. She had had a front-row seat to the way his parents' marriage worked and it was…*sad*. They spoke without warmth to each other, as if they were inquiring about a telephone bill minus the anxiety that they might struggle to pay. "What kind of marriage would that be as an example for her?"

"A calm and rational one?" he suggested.

"I don't want rational! I want what my grandparents had." She waved wildly in the direction of the house where she had witnessed deep, abiding love, every single day. "I want pet names for each other and a love that endures through a lifetime."

"You want me to call you red?"

"Don't make fun of me. Or them," she warned. "Gran stayed in that drafty house an extra year for Gramps, because she knew it would break his heart to leave it. Now she can't stand to sleep in it without him there beside her."

"And you want that?" He sounded askance.

"It beats being married to a stranger. Occupying a mausoleum of a house while pursuing separate lives."

"My parents' marriage is an alliance based on shared values. That's not a bad thing if you agree on those values beforehand."

"Speaking from experience, are you?"

Another harsh silence descended. This time she regretted her words. His pregnant wife had died. He might not have loved Faustina, but it must be a very raw wound.

Recalling that, her suspicions of his motives

arose again. Maybe he would come to care for Lily, but why was he here now? What did he *really* want?

"Rico... You understand that one baby cannot replace another, don't you?" She knew she had to tread softly on that one, but couldn't hold that apprehension inside her. "If that's why you're here, then no." It broke her heart to deny Lily her father, but, "I won't let you do that to Lily."

He stiffened and she braced herself for his scathing reaction, but it wasn't at all what she expected.

"Faustina's baby wasn't *mine*."

CHAPTER FOUR

THE WORDS WERE supposed to stay inside his head, but they resounded across the crisp air. Through the trees and off the sky. They made icicles drop like knives and stab into the frozen snow.

From a long way away, he heard Poppy say a hollow and breathless, "What?" Her thin, strained voice was no louder than his own had been, but rang like a gong in his ears.

He pinched the bridge of his nose, the leather of his gloves cold. All of him was encased in the dry ice of Canadian winter while his blood pumped in thick lumps through his arteries. His chest tightened and his shoulders ached.

"I shouldn't have said that. We should get back." He glanced the way they'd come, but it was shorter if she would only keep moving ahead on the path.

Thankfully, he couldn't see a soul. They were the only pair of fools out here stumbling through the dark. He waved for her to proceed.

"Rico." Her mitted hand came onto his forearm. "Is that true?"

The quaver in her voice matched the conscience still wobbling like a dropped coin in the pit of his stomach.

"Forget I said it. I mean it, Poppy."

"I can't." She didn't let him brush away her grip on his sleeve. *"It matters.* Tell me."

"If I tell you…" He shifted so he cupped her elbow, holding her before him. "It stays between us. *Forever.* Do you understand?"

He had already said too much, but she was the mother of his child. His *actual* child. He had only tentatively absorbed that knowledge, only enough to know that one way or another he would bring them both back to Spain with him. Marriage was the quickest, most practical means of doing that. Therefore, she deserved to know the truth about his first marriage. As his wife, he expected her to protect his secrets as closely as he would guard hers.

And, damn it, he felt as though he'd been holding his breath for a thousand years. He couldn't contain it one minute longer.

"Her parents found her," he said, overcome with pity for them, despite his bitterness at Faustina's lies. The colossal waste of life couldn't be denied. The unborn baby might not have been his, but he was a decent enough human being to feel sadness and regret that it had been as much a victim as its parents.

"Where?" Poppy asked with dread.

"The garage. It wasn't deliberate. They'd packed bags, had train tickets. She was with her parents' chauffeur, naked in the back seat. They must have made love, perhaps started the car to warm it, then fallen asleep. They never woke up. Carbon monoxide poisoning."

"Oh, my God." She covered her mouth. "That's *horrible*."

"Yes. Her parents were devastated. Still

are. They didn't know about the affair. They begged me to keep it under wraps."

"So you've been letting everyone think— How do you know the baby wasn't yours?"

"I had the coroner run tests."

"You told me that day you two weren't sleeping together." She twitched in his grip.

He released her. His palm felt cold, even inside his glove. He was solid ice, all the way to his core, still playing what-ifs in his head.

"Do you think *she* knew it wasn't yours?" she asked tentatively.

"Of course she knew," he spat with the contempt he felt for himself as much as for Faustina. "I had already begun to suspect. As soon as they found her, I knew what she had done. We *weren't* sleeping together. We made love *once* during our engagement. Faustina insisted. Said she wanted to be sure we'd be a good fit. After that, there were excuses. Headaches. Finally she said we should wait until the ceremony, to make our wedding night more exciting."

He hadn't argued. The first experience had

barely moved him, certainly hadn't rocked his world the way another very memorable experience had. He skimmed his gaze over Poppy's face, so ghostly in the moonlight.

He'd told himself things would improve with Faustina once they got to know one another. He hadn't realized yet that it was possible to fall into immersive pleasure so profound he could be transported from the world around him. So much so that he made love with a woman he barely knew in the near-public solarium and had thought about her every day since.

He ran his gloved hand over his face. The seam in his palm scraped his skin, allowing him to focus on the rest of the ugly story.

"I believe she learned she was pregnant and slept with me so she could pass the baby off as mine."

"When?"

He knew what she was asking. "A few weeks before she broke things off with me on the day you and I were together."

Poppy rubbed her arm where he'd held her elbow.

"I've since learned that when she left my parents' house, she went straight to her own and told them she had called off the wedding. Her father threatened to disinherit her. They're very faithful and strict, demanded she abide by the agreement. They would have fired the driver if they'd had any inkling of her reason. Maybe even sued him for damages or destroyed him in some other way. Faustina's choice was to live destitute with her lover or crawl back to me."

It was the only explanation for how a stable, well-bred, otherwise honest woman could have behaved in such an underhanded way.

"A week before they died, she used her settlement from our marriage to close on a small house in the north of Spain, near his relatives. That's where they were headed."

"That's so…sad."

"Sad and sordid and I torture myself every day wondering if she would be alive if I'd refused to marry her that next morning."

"Why did you agree? The presidency?" Her voice panged in a way that grated against his conscience. The opportunity to run Faustina's father's company, proving himself in his own arena away from Cesar's shadow, had been the carrot that drew him into the engagement, but it wouldn't have enticed him to go through with the wedding the second time.

"She said she'd just found out she was pregnant, that it was the reason she'd been so emotional the day before. She said the baby was from that *one time*—when I used a condom, by the way. I should have suspected she was lying, but…" Here were the what-ifs. What if he had asked more questions, balked, told her he'd slept with the maid? That he'd *liked* it.

He hadn't done any of that. He'd done his duty by his family. He had done what was expected because, "I thought the baby was *mine.*"

"When did you start to suspect it wasn't?"

"The wedding night. She didn't want to have sex. Said the pregnancy was turning her off." Rico had been nursing his own regrets and hadn't pressed her. "She was very moody. Conflicted, obviously. And putting her ducks in a row to leave me. We never did sleep together again. Things grew strained as I realized she was keeping something from me. I put off a confrontation, but it was coming. Then I got the call from her father."

"I'm so sorry, Rico. It's truly awful that you've had to carry this."

"I don't want your pity, Poppy." He curled his hands into fists, straining the seams in his gloves. "I want your silence. I expect it. Not even Cesar knows and we don't keep much from one another. But I swore to her parents I'd keep it quiet."

"What about the company?"

"Her father asked me to stay on as President. He's sickened that she tricked me. I could weather the scandal if the truth came out, but it would destroy them. Despite Faustina's behavior, they're good people. I don't want to hurt them any more than they have been."

"I'll never say a word," she promised.

He nodded, believing her because they were in this together now.

"You understand why I told you? If she had been honest and up front about her situation, I would have helped her, maybe even raised that baby if she had asked me to. I wouldn't have punished the child for her failings." His anger returned, making his nostrils sting. "But I don't appreciate that you have also kept secrets from me, Poppy."

He heard her breath catch as though he'd struck her.

"I will *not* ignore my actual blood. I want *my* daughter."

She took a step back, but he caught her arm, keeping her close and tilting his head to peer through the shadows straight into her eyes.

"You *will* come to Spain. You *will* marry me and we will make this work."

Poppy might have knocked his hand away if she hadn't needed his touch to steady her; his words were that impactful.

"That's a big leap," she managed shakily.

"I won't keep you from knowing her, Rico. I see why Lily being yours has extra significance for you." Her heart was aching under the weight of what he'd revealed and she had only just heard it. It had been festering in him for nearly two years. "But you and I barely know each other."

"We know each other," he scoffed gently. "I just told you something I haven't told *anyone*."

And she had shared her heartache over her parents' neglect.

A similar thing had happened that day in the solarium. Their conversation had somehow become deeply personal. Her crush on him had been instant and she'd never meant it to become obvious to him, but for weeks she had longed to talk to him in a meaningful way. She had wanted to find out who he was beneath his shell of gorgeous looks, easy manners and unsmudged armor.

She recalled telling him about that liar of a backpacker who had stolen everything she had, then asked why he had agreed to an arranged marriage.

Why compete with a business rival if a marriage can turn them into a partner? Faustina's very upstanding family would never connect themselves so intimately to any but the most exemplary politician, which polishes my father's already stellar reputation in the upper house of Parliament. Faustina gains the social standing of marrying into a titled family. My mother gets the heiress and the wedding event she envisioned for my brother.

It had seemed so laughably factual. She had asked him what he stood to gain and he'd mentioned running a company he would control, allowing him to pursue ambitions away from working for his brother.

A rational part of her brain had warned her that she deserved someone better than a man bouncing off a broken engagement, but her pride had needed the focused attention of someone so much grander than she was. She had thought the camera thief had genuinely liked her, but he'd been flattering her to blind her. Rico hadn't wanted anything from her except *her.* If he was rebounding after his own rejection, that was okay. It was one more detail that made them equals.

And when their kisses had escalated with passion, she hadn't wanted to stop. His love-making had been exactly what she had needed in that moment. Much as she believed she would only marry for love, she had known a soul-mate connection was an elusive thing. Expecting the full package of love and plea-sure and a lifelong commitment for her first time wasn't realistic.

It had been enough to have infatuation and a man who ought to be firmly out of her reach, but who brought her entire body to life by simply watching the release of a button on her dress, then lifting his gaze to check in with her as his finger traced a caress against her skin.

She put a halt to recalling the rest or she'd succumb to him all over again without so much as a single protest.

"This is the second time we've spoken," she

pointed out, inwardly shaking at how profound their encounters had been. "We made love *once*."

"With spectacular results." His gloved hand took hold of her chin. "I'm not just talking about Lily."

She was so glad he couldn't see her blush, but her helplessness was on full display in her strained voice. "That was... You were relieved you weren't marrying," she accused. "Coming off a dry spell with the first woman you happened across."

"I noticed you before that."

They were close enough that the fog of their breath was mingling.

"I wouldn't have kissed you if you hadn't made a point of telling me you'd finished your last shift and were no longer an employee," he reminded. "The attraction was mutual."

"I didn't make a *point* of it." Maybe she had. He had asked if she wanted to leave and had moved aside, giving her plenty of space to walk past him to the change rooms where she'd been headed when she had bumped into him. She had stayed, eager to keep talking to him. Basking in the glory of being noticed by him.

"Do you ever think about that day?" he asked.

Constantly. She wouldn't admit it, though.

"Hmm?" he prompted, lowering his head. He stopped before he kissed her.

She let her eyes flutter closed and parted her lips in invitation.

He only grazed his mouth against hers, provoking a buzzing sensation in her lips.

She put out a hand, but the knit of her mitten only found the smooth leather of his jacket, too slippery to hold on to.

While he kept up that frustratingly light tickle. His hand shifted to cup the side of her neck, the rough seam on his thumb grazing the tender skin in her throat.

"Do you?" He refused to give her what she wanted until she answered.

Her skin grew too tight for the anticipation that swelled within her. Beneath the layers of her thick jacket, her breasts grew heavy.

Her thighs ceased to feel the cold through the denim of her jeans.

"Yes," she admitting on a throb of longing.

He made a noise of satisfaction and stepped so his feet were outside her own. His hot mouth sealed across her lips.

A sob of delight broke in her throat as his hard lips raked across hers, making real all the erotic fantasies she'd replayed in the long nights since leaving Spain. Her arms went up around his neck and he swept her closer still. So close she could hardly breathe.

She didn't care. The thick layers of their coats were a frustration, one that seemed to hold them off from one another. She wanted them *gone*. Wanted passion to take her over the way it had that day, blanking out the world around her with levels of excitement and pleasure she hadn't known existed.

His kiss deepened with greed, as though he couldn't get enough of her, either. She opened fully to him, licked into his mouth and felt his arms tighten around her in response. She ran her hand up past his scarf, pressed the back of his head, urging him to kiss her harder and harder still. She wanted him to mark her. Savage her.

Because he already had.

This passion between them was as destructive as it was glorious. She needed to remember that. Otherwise, she would succumb and wind up far out of her depth again.

As though he recognized the risk as well, he dragged his head up and sucked in a breath, but he didn't let her go.

Panting, she blinked her eyes open. His face was in darkness with a kaleidoscope of colors haloed behind him.

"Look." She seized the distraction to pull herself out of his arms. She wasn't even sure if what she was seeing was real or the leftover fireworks he had so easily set off behind her eyelids.

She staggered slightly as she led him out of the trees. The expanse of sky was bigger than a thousand movie screens above them and the stars had faded behind glowing swirls. Shimmering bands of pink and purple and red danced within the curtains of green. Every few seconds a spear of color shot toward the earth in knifelike streaks. The jabs of color felt so tangible and close, she expected to be struck by one.

"This is beautiful." Rico drew her back against his chest and folded his arms across her collarbone and stomach.

She was still weak from their kiss. She leaned into the wall he made, wondering if he could feel the thump of her still unsteady heart through their winter layers.

"One of my first memories is coming out here with my grandfather," she confided softly. "I asked when my mother was coming back and he brought me out here. I thought he was going to tell me she had died. He said he didn't know if she was coming back, but then he pointed to the sky. I asked what it was and he said he didn't know that, either. That there would always be things in this world we're left to wonder about."

"Gas particles from the sun collide with the earth's atmosphere," Rico informed her.

"Don't ruin it." She nudged her elbow back into his ribs. "It's *magic*. I've taken a million photographs of them, but none capture how amazing this really is. How small it makes you feel."

"I've never seen it like this." His chin touched the top of her head.

"Me, neither." This was the most glorious display she'd ever witnessed and she didn't care that she didn't have her camera. She would never forget sharing this with him: the timbre of his voice vibrating through her jacket, the heat of his breath against her ear-lobe where it poked from beneath her toque, the weight of his arm across her and the way all those colors glowed inside her even as they danced before her unblinking eyes.

She hesitated then confessed softly, "Gramps brought me out here when I was pregnant, too. I wanted to keep Lily, but I didn't know how I would manage it. It felt too much of an imposition to stay with them. He was upset that he wouldn't be around to look after me and Gran. We had a little cry then saw these lights. He said it was a reminder that even dark nights offer beautiful moments and said that's what Lily would be for all of us if I stayed with them."

Rico's arm tightened across her chest. His voice was low and sincere. "I'm sorry I didn't meet him."

Her chest ached. "I think that's him right now."

A startled pause, then, "I don't believe in things like that, Poppy."

"It's okay." She touched the arm that continued to hold her close. "I do."

"If I did—" His lips pressed to her ear through the knit of her toque. "I think we both know what he's saying."

Her throat grew tight. *Marry Rico.*

He drew back slightly so he could reach into his jacket. When he brought his hand around in front of her, he held a small box. He stayed behind her as he pried up the lid so she stood in the circle of his arms as he offered her the ring.

The band could have been silver or yellow

or rose. The diamond caught glints of colored light, blinding her.

Had he really come all this way, not knowing for sure if Lily was his, but brought a ring just in case?

She let him pick up her left hand and tug at the mitten. She took the discarded mitt with her free hand. As though under a spell, she turned to face him.

She tried to think of reasons to persuade him this was wrong or stupid or doomed to fail. Marrying him was all of those things.

But she wanted to marry him. Her compulsion to know him remained. Beneath the anger and armor of indifference was a man who wanted to know his daughter. That meant everything to her.

As the aurora borealis continued to crash silently over them, full of mystical power and spirit voices, she told herself that Gramps wouldn't steer her wrong. He wouldn't tell her to marry Rico if this would ruin her life. He was telling her to say goodbye to her home and family and begin building her new one.

The cool ring caught slightly on her knuckle, then it was on her finger, heavy as the promise it symbolized. Rico's mouth came down to hers again with magnificent heat, burning away her bleak doubts and fears, filling her with hope and possibility.

CHAPTER FIVE

You should have told me sooner. I would have made arrangements. Someone from the family should have been there.

Rico read the text from Pia and swore, then dropped the phone onto the custom recliner beside the one he occupied.

Across from him, buckled into her own, Poppy looked up from distracting Lily with a book. Lily was making noises of dismay at being strapped into her car seat while the view beyond the windows turned to clouds.

"What's wrong?" Poppy asked him.

"A text from my sister, scolding me about the wedding."

"She's upset?" Poppy's expression dimmed.

"That I didn't invite her. I pointed out there hasn't been time."

It hadn't occurred to him Pia would want to come. His parents had urged him to wait for the DNA results and expressed consternation that he hadn't. Cesar's reaction to his impending nuptials had been a curt text.

Sorcha told me. Congratulations.

Rico had given up at that point and focused on the tasks at hand.

Poppy's gran had been moved to her sister's apartment, where she would occupy a guest room for a few days. Rico had had to push to make it happen, but he had arranged to have her personal items moved into a nearby, private seniors' complex that was so well-appointed, Eleanor had asked him if he'd won a lottery.

Poppy had been anxious about the entire process until she'd spoken with the extremely personable, on-staff doctor who had already been in touch with her grandmother's specialist. A nutritionist had made note of her grandmother's dislike of cumin. Her sensitivity to certain detergents had been conveyed to the housekeeping staff. Eleanor had looked in on the pool where physical therapy sessions were held and checked out the lively games room, approving the entire complex with a delighted nod.

Poppy's father had pointed out that the location in Regina would be easier for him to visit, too. He typically spent half a day driving after his flight landed. Rico had even hired a caretaker to look after the house until decisions had been made on whether to keep it in the family.

The last task had been a brief civil service at the courthouse. Poppy's father had given her away and her grandmother had wept happy tears. They had eaten brunch at an upscale café then climbed aboard his private jet.

Another text rang through, but he ignored it.

"Tell her I didn't even have my mother there," Poppy said.

"I explained why I was keeping it private."

"That wasn't a complaint," she said stiffly, making him aware of how tersely he'd spoken.

"I didn't *want* my mother there." She picked up the book Lily dropped, mouth pinched.

Poppy had said she would inform her mother after Rico issued the press release. He'd had enough to juggle in the moment that he hadn't questioned her. Now he did.

"Why not?" Had she been afraid she wouldn't show up? Her mother sounded even less emotionally accessible than his own. At least La Reina Montero maintained appearances.

"I was afraid she wouldn't keep her mouth shut," Poppy muttered crossly. "I agree with you that it's kinder to let your parents inform Faustina's parents and give them a few days to prepare their own statement."

Loathe as he was to bring Faustina into this marriage on any level, he appreciated Poppy's understanding. Having a child Lily's age wouldn't reflect well on his fidelity, narrow window of a called-off wedding notwithstanding. This news would come as a shock to many, including Faustina's parents.

"I didn't mean to speak sharply. I don't usually make mistakes and they've been piling up lately."

For the most part, Rico was a meticulous planner. He had always been taught success was a matter of research and preparation. That lesson had played out as true more often than not and he had heeded its wisdom—right up until he had impulsively made love with his mother's maid.

He had promptly fallen back in line with the precisely orchestrated pageant his first wedding had been, only to discover his wife's betrayal. As resentful as he still was of that, he had to face the fact that if he had refused to marry Faustina when she had come back that next morning, she might be alive and happily ensconced with her lover and child. He wouldn't have the presidency that had seemed like such a delectable consolation prize, but he would have had the first year of Lily's life. Poppy bore some responsibility for his missing that, but so did he.

He had believed his tryst with Poppy was all the bucking of expectations he had needed before settling into the life laid out for him. Even after Sorcha had dropped this earth-shattering news on him, he had attempted to defuse it with surgical care, ordering an investigation and telling no one.

Then the test had come back inconclusive and he had come out of his skin. Mere days later, he had a wife and child. His parents thought he was behaving recklessly and a rational part of him wondered if they were right. He was relying on instinct without concrete evidence or other facts to back it up.

He caught Poppy's affronted glare and heard his own words.

"I wasn't suggesting this marriage is a mistake. But it will cause a tragic death to be splashed across the gossip sites again. *You* will be cast as the Other Woman."

She would be labeled an opportunist and a gold digger. Given her shock at his arrival, he couldn't accuse her of that, but others would.

"I'll look like a faithless husband and a deadbeat father. I'm not proud of any of that.

Scandals are not my MO. I'm disgusted with myself for creating this situation."

"And what about Lily? Are you sorry you created her?" The fiery challenge in her expression was quickly schooled as the flight attendant approached to ask after their comfort.

Lily lifted her arms at the woman and pitifully begged, "Oof?"

"She thinks that means up," Poppy explained with a stiff smile. "I guess I was making that noise whenever I lifted her and didn't notice. Button, you have to stay in your seat. I'll apologize now for how miserable she's going to become."

Rico preferred a happy baby over one who was screaming, same as anyone. The baby in question, however, was his. He hadn't fully unpacked that knowledge and very tentatively felt around in the dank spaces within him, looking for the regret Poppy had accused him of feeling toward Lily.

"Our flight should be very smooth until we're over the Atlantic," the attendant said.

"She could walk around if you want to let her work out some energy."

"She doesn't walk yet."

"There isn't much she can get into," Rico pointed out, still searching through the bitterness that encased him for resentment that was wrongly aimed at an innocent child. "All the drawers have catches so they won't open midflight."

Poppy peered at the floors. They were as spotless as they ought to be, given the salaries he paid his flight crews.

"You really wouldn't mind?" Poppy asked the attendant.

"Of course not." The attendant was bemused by the question and disappeared to fetch the coffee he requested.

Poppy heard his snort and shot him a frown as she unstrapped Lily. "Why am I funny?"

"This is my plane. If my daughter wants to pilot it through loop-de-loops, it's the crew's job to make it happen." That much he *was* sure of.

Poppy released a small oof of exertion as she

pulled Lily out of her seat and stood her on the floor, next to her knee. Then she reached into the toy bag and handed Lily a giraffe. She tossed the half-dozen other toys onto the empty seat next to Rico.

Lily reached for the bag, needing to peek inside to see if more would appear.

"It's empty. They're all there," Poppy told her, pointing.

Lily dropped the giraffe, let go of Poppy's knee and took three toddling steps, completely unassisted.

Poppy gasped and reached out to catch her, but Lily slapped her dimpled hand onto Rico's knee. Her fingers closed like kitten claws into the fabric of his trousers as she steadied herself. Then she cruised around his leg and began examining the array of toys.

Poppy clapped her hand over her open mouth. Her eyes brimmed with excited tears. "Did you see that?" She dropped her hand, but emotion husked her voice.

"Those weren't her *first* steps." It couldn't be. There'd been no fanfare. No announcement over the PA that it was about to happen. It had occurred naturally, as if she'd been doing it all along.

Poppy nodded like a bobblehead doll on the dash of a derby car.

"They were. Just like that. Baby is gone and she's a toddler." She wiped her damp eyes. "I shouldn't be so silly about it. Gran kept saying it would happen any day."

Lily had found his phone amid the stuffed toys and plastic keys. He started to take it from her, but a fierce swell of pride moved his hand to her hair. He faltered briefly then grazed his palm lightly over her fine red hair, downy as a duckling.

She was such a tiny, perfect little human. Recognizing how vulnerable she was made his heart clench in a strange panic. An urge to protect rose in him, but he already knew he wouldn't be sufficient to the task. Not forever. Things would happen beyond his control. Then what? He had instinctively shied from this depth of responsibility, but here it was, thrust upon him, heavy and unavoidable, yet oddly welcome.

How could he not want to shield such a precious young life? How could he ever blame her for existing?

"You don't have to impress me, you know," he told Lily, rueful that he was so button-bursting proud of three little steps.

Lily grinned and held up his phone.

"Thank you," he said politely and pocketed the item, offering a teething ring in exchange. He shifted his attention to Poppy.

"We both could have handled many things better," he told her, clearing his voice to steady it while he mentally allowed the cloak of fatherhood to settle more comfortably over his shoulders. "But I will never, ever regard Lily as a mistake."

Rico gently transferred Lily into a blue crib that likely belonged to Mateo. Rico had said this darkened penthouse in Madrid was used by any member of the family who happened to have business in the capital.

Poppy carefully tucked blankets around her overtired little girl. The first half of the flight had gone well. Everyone had caught a few hours of sleep, but Lily had begun fussing when turbulence forced her to be strapped back into her seat. By the time she had cried herself out and begun to nod off, they were descending and her ears were popping, upsetting her all over again.

"I think she's down for the count," Poppy said with relief as they stepped out of the room.

Rico clicked on the baby monitor and brought it with them into the lounge where he turned on a few lamps. He moved with casual confidence, hardly a wrinkle in his clothes, his eyes heavy-lidded and inscrutable.

"Are you hungry?"

"No. I feel like all I did was eat on the flight." She crossed her arms and hunched her shoulders, hyperaware that they were alone for the first time since they'd stood under the stars that first night.

They were also married.

She had heard him tell the driver to leave their luggage in *his* room, but there was a conversation they needed to have before they shared it. She hadn't figured out yet how to broach it. She wished she could be blasé and sophisticated, but she felt callow and fearful of his reaction. Would he laugh? Look at her with disappointment?

"I…um…wouldn't mind a shower," she murmured, more for a chance to be alone and clear her head.

"Do you want company?" His voice lowered, growing thick with sensual invitation.

Her stomach took a rollercoaster dip and swirl while a wave of heat pushed out from her center, leaving her fingers and toes, nipples and scalp all tingling.

She wanted to laugh at how easily he segued into addressing the elephant, but some of her trepidation must have shown. His expression tightened.

"We don't have to if you're tired."

"It's not that," she murmured, more wired than tired, still trying to come to terms with everything that had happened in such a whirl-wind. Drawing a breath of courage, she said, "I'm not sure what you expect."

A brief pulse of surprise, then he said stiffly, "I expect this marriage to include a sexual re-lationship. I'll never force it, though. And I would normally say a woman doesn't need an excuse for turning me down, but given Faus-tina's reasons, I'd like to understand yours."

"I'm not turning you down," she said with a small, nervous smile that wouldn't stick. "I expected we'd have sex. When I took Lily for her blood test the other day, I left her with the nurse so I could get an IUD." Sometimes her hair gifted her with the clichéd fiery blushes and now was one of those times. The entire room should have turned bordello red, she glowed so hotly with the admission that she had premeditated having sex with him.

He frowned. "You don't want more chil-dren?"

"Not right away." Her cheeks hurt, they were scorched so deeply. "This is a lot to get used to, don't you think? Without bringing a newborn into the mix?"

He tipped his head slightly, acknowledging the point, but a hint of suspicion glinted in his narrowed eyes. Perhaps he saw the rest of the logic that had propelled her decision—a new baby would make it more difficult for her to leave if she had to.

"I want this marriage to work," she assured him. "But there are things…" Her voice failed her. She cleared her throat. "Things we should discuss before…"

"Health concerns?"

"You mean disease? No! I'm perfectly fine. Are you—?"

"Completely fine," he clipped out. "I was asking if there were complications with delivering Lily that affected you?"

"No. Just the usual leftover imperfections of stretch marks and… Well, you can see I'm still carrying a bit of baby weight. Lily weaned herself three months ago and apparently these aren't going away." She waved at the chest that remained a cup size bigger than prepregnancy.

"I assure you I don't consider any of those things 'imperfections.' Particularly the added curves. Is that the source of your hesitation? You're self-conscious? We can keep the lights off if it will make you more comfortable. I'd prefer it, too. Otherwise my scar from my appendix surgery might turn you off."

"Why would— Oh. All right, I get your point." She rolled her eyes.

He paced closer, which made her freeze in place, skin growing tight with anticipation while nervous butterflies filled her torso, swirling around in every direction.

He touched her chin, coaxing her to meet his gaze with her own. "We've done this before," he reminded her.

"About that…" She clasped his flat wrist and squeezed her eyes shut. "That's the only time I've had sex. Ever."

She felt the flex in his wrist and the slight increase of pressure in his grip on her chin.

"Open your eyes," he commanded, voice

seeming to resonate from the depths of his chest.

She did, meeting his gaze with chagrin. She wasn't ashamed of being a virgin so much as feeling guilty for having misled him that day.

All she could see were his eyes, iridescent almost. Like granite that revealed flecks of precious gems when wet, glints of blue and green in the gray surrounding a giant black pool. His pupils were huge. Atavistic.

Yet skeptical.

"*Ever*," she reiterated helplessly.

Rico couldn't think of another time he'd been utterly speechless. Not that his mind had the capacity to filter any moments other than the one she was referring to. The shyness of her hands squeezing him through his pants and fumbling with his belt.

Enthusiasm counted for more than expertise when it came to lovemaking. If he'd given any thought to her lack of finesse, he had likely imagined she was as overcome as he was. He couldn't say his own performance had been particularly adept, given the stolen nature of their tryst.

He remembered clearly that moment afterward, though, when his lingering pleasure had dimmed because he had feared he had hurt her.

Is your cycle starting?

I guess. Sorry. She'd been mortified.

Don't apologize. At least we're safe from—

He'd been appalled at forgetting the condom. He *never* forgot.

"I don't like lies," he warned her now, lips numb. This news was melting his face off his skull.

"I'm being honest." She winced as though she was squirming inside. "I want to sleep with you, but I don't want you to be…" She swallowed. Her voice remained strained. "Disappointed. *I* don't want to be disappointed."

The word wafted over him, so far from what he might be feeling as to be incomprehensible. Then his ego absorbed the hit.

"Were *you* disappointed that day?"

"No." She withdrew from him a few steps and crossed her arms.

But she had nothing to compare it to. Her lack of experience began to penetrate. Belated concern struck. They'd been quite passionate. "Did I hurt you?"

"No. I mean, a little, but not…" She looked to the ceiling as though seeking deliverance. "I was fine with the discomfort. There were compensations," she added with a small groan of embarrassed irony.

"You felt pleasure?" He had to know. "You weren't faking your enjoyment, were you? Did you climax? Because I thought you did, but—"

"Are we really doing a forensic audit on it?" she cried, face so red it should have been accompanied by five alarms.

"I need to know, Poppy." It was imperative.

"I didn't fake anything! Okay? Quit asking such personal questions."

"How is this too personal? We were both there and I'm making sure we were both *there*. My pride is every bit as delicate as any man's.

When it comes to the bedroom, if you're not satisfied, I'm not satisfied. I will make you that promise right now."

She ducked her eyes into her hand. "Thanks. And I'd love to make the same promise, but *I don't know what I'm doing*."

"You don't have to be defensive about it. I'm glad you told me. And your number of past lovers is far less important to me than how many you have *now*." Obviously. "Shall we agree we'll keep it to one?"

She peered at him over her hand, admonishing, but also earnest as she promised, "Of course I'll be monogamous."

"Thank you. So will I." But he was still having trouble believing she had shelved all her passion once she'd discovered it. "There really hasn't been anyone since me?"

"Who would I sleep with, pregnant out to here?" She set her hand in the air beyond her navel. "I was looking after my grandparents and a newborn. Babies make you want to have a date with your pillow and no one else, trust me."

She looked too uncomfortable to be telling him anything but the truth.

It was starting to impact him that the most profound sexual experience of his life had been with a virgin. He wasn't sentimental, but there was something endearing in knowing he was her only lover.

"Why me?" he asked gently. "Why that day?"

"Because I was feeling like my whole trip had been a bust and I wanted one decent memory to take home with me."

"I was a *souvenir*?"

"I was just a notch on your belt, wasn't I?" she shot back.

His heart lurched and he had to look away, thinking of the way he had obsessed about her ever since. He had tried to relegate her to a notch. Instead, she'd been another persistent what-if.

"It's fine that you were only taking what I offered," she said, hugging herself. "I didn't care that you had all the experience and seduced me. I wanted you to. But now you're only having sex with me because we're married and you're stuck with me. That would be fine if I felt like I was bringing something to the table, but I don't have any sexual confidence because I've only done it *one time*." Her brow furrowed.

Aside from the chaste kiss after the ceremony, he hadn't touched her since their kiss under the stars, but he'd been acutely aware of her every minute since she had opened her door to him. His ears were attuned to each inflection in her voice—the chuckling remarks she exchanged with her grandmother, the loving tone she used when speaking to Lily. He had studied the fit of her jeans, drunk in the scent of her hair, enjoyed the smooth warmth of her hand if their fingers happened to touch. He had noted the way her lips closed over a fork and the little frown that appeared between her brows if she was growing stubborn.

He had spent every night lying awake, recalling their passionate union until he was so filled with ardor, he ached.

He couldn't believe she didn't know that.

But he had taken pains to keep his reaction hidden so as not to let her undermine him with what he perceived as a weakness. He hadn't wanted to admit that he had obsessed about her from the first moment he'd seen her dusting his mother's furniture.

"You have a lot to compare to and I don't want to start our marriage by falling short of your expectations." She offered a dejected smile. "That's why we're standing here instead of in the shower."

CHAPTER SIX

POPPY FELT LIKE a head case and was trying not to apologize for it. Women were allowed to have reservations. To feel conflicted. She might want sex, but she didn't want empty sex. Not this time. Not when she had tried that the first time and discovered she wasn't capable of keeping her emotions out of the experience.

But Rico was her husband and the father of her child and their kisses had reassured her that their lovemaking would be as pleasurable as it had been the first time.

Maybe she was expecting too much.

Was that what he was thinking behind that enigmatic expression? A muscle was pulsing in his jaw as though he was trying to crack nuts with his teeth.

"I haven't been with anyone else, either," he finally said.

"Oh, please." Disappointment in him descended like a curtain while her heart latched a little too hard on to that outrageous statement. "It's been nearly two years!" He could have his pick of supermodels. He'd gotten the maid with a wink and a smile, hadn't he?

"I already told you that I slept with Faustina *once*. Weeks before you." He opened his eyes to scowl with affront at her distrust. "I didn't cheat on her, and given the way my marriage ended, I haven't been feeling very amorous."

She found that believable, actually.

"Until very recently," he added pointedly, pretty much flinging sexual awareness at her and leaving her coated in it. "All of which could impact *my* performance. You're not the only one with high stakes here."

"Oh, I'm sure we're on exactly the same level of nerves," she muttered sarcastically.

He relaxed slightly, eyeing her. "Do you think about it?"

"What? Sex?" The whole world tilted like a

magnifying glass. One moment certain things had loomed large, now all of that went out of focus while a bright ray of heat singed into her bones. "With you, or…?"

"Anyone. But sure, me."

She was *not* going to admit that she thought about him *all the time*. "I can't believe you're asking me these things."

"This is exactly the sort of conversation a husband and wife should be able to have."

"Do *you*?" she challenged.

"Think about you? Of course. I've often re-called our lovemaking and imagined doing things with you that we didn't have time to enjoy."

He was admitting to fantasizing about her. And he wasn't flinching in the least. He was staring right into her eyes and making *her* think of things she wished they'd done.

His brow went up in a light challenge.

She swallowed, hot all over.

"I imagine you're in the shower with me. For instance," he provided in a drawl that somehow pulled all her nerve endings tight.

"If you're looking for a seductive move, I guarantee you an invitation to join you will always pique my interest."

She narrowed her eyes. "I don't appreciate you making fun of me."

"I'm not joking," he assured her, but amusement lurked around his mouth.

"Fine," she said with annoyance. "Let's move this to the shower, then."

"Poppy."

His voice caught like a hook in her heart, pulling her around without even touching her before she could hurry down the hall.

She caught her breath. If he said he didn't want to, she might lose her nerve and never find it again.

"What?" she demanded when he waited until she quit spinning her gaze around the room in avoidance and made herself look at him.

"This isn't a test." His voice grew grave. Tense. "If you're not ready, say so."

"I said I want to!" She waved in the direction she'd been headed.

He came toward her, brows raised in a mild scold. "You're nervous. Maybe instead of barreling into the shower, we should slow down."

"I want the awkwardness over with," she admitted, bordering on petulant.

He gently peeled her hands off her elbows and held them in a loose grip. "But if I'd been in less of a hurry last time, I might have noticed you were new to this. *I* want to be sure you're with me every step. Why don't we start with a kiss?"

"Really?" She rolled her eyes toward the ceiling. "Fine. If that's what you want."

"Humor me." He stepped in and stole a single kiss, one of those deliberately light ones that made desire soak through her like gasoline.

She shifted lightly on her feet, instantly restless, but not in a hurry to go anywhere. "You could try that again."

He did, lingering. Taking his time finding the right fit, playing with levels of pressure.

While she shyly returned his kiss, her whole body became sensitized to everything around them. The lamplight chasing them toward the hall, the scent of faint cologne against his cheek and the slight rustle of their clothing as they stopped holding hands and reached to touch. Her hand came to rest on the fabric of his shirt, curling into a fist that crushed the fine linen while her mouth moved with tremulous passion beneath his, encouraging him.

That bashful invitation seemed to test his control. He growled and deepened the kiss. His hands found her waist and drew her fully against him.

All the memories she had convinced herself were fantasy were becoming real. He was here. She was in his arms, in his home. This was her new life. It was too much. A small cry sounded in her throat.

He lifted his head. Both of them tried to steady their breath.

She suddenly remembered him saying, *You deserve better than the lowlife who took your camera.*

She had known she did, but she hadn't believed she deserved him. Not for more than a brief hour. At the time, she had countered, *She didn't deserve you, either. I hope you find someone better.* She had wanted him to see *her* as an option. To *want* her.

Did he? She could tell he was affected by their kiss, but he was pulling himself back under control as she watched.

This was the true source of her apprehension. That she would lose herself to his touch again and whatever grip or autonomy she had over her life would slip away. After their first time, even before she had learned she was pregnant, she had known her life would never be the same. Every other man would be compared to him and fall short.

After tonight, he would know he could do this to her. He could break down her barriers without effort, own her body and soul. Her eyes began to sting at her defenselessness.

His hands moved soothingly across her lower back. His eyes had gone more blue than gray and were shot with sparks of green, hot as the center of a flame. As he slowly drew her in again, he made a noise that was a question.

She settled gladly against him. Melted into him.

If she had had the strength of mind, of willpower, she might have balked. But she wanted this. She craved his touch like she'd been sucked into quicksand and suddenly found the vine that would pull her free.

He lowered his head and took another thorough taste of her, long and lazy and luscious. The stab of his tongue acted like alcohol, shooting pleasurable trickles of heat through her veins. She grew loose of limb and warm and weak. She moaned softly and curled her arms around his neck, encouraging him.

He settled into a passionate kiss, not aggressive, but full of confidence. Unhurried and possessive. Seductive.

She quit thinking about whether she was being reckless or not skilled enough. She let herself sink into the play of his mouth across hers and simply feel. Feel the hardness of him with her whole body as she rose on her tip-toes. Feel the silk of his hair with her fingers and the faint abrasion of chin stubble as he twisted his head and swept his tongue across hers.

She immersed herself in the feel of *him*. The sweep of his hands across her back and down to her hips, the iron thighs holding steady as she leaned into him. The erotic hardness of his erection pressing into her abdomen, telling her she was affecting him.

The knowledge he was aroused sent arrows of answering lust deep into her belly. Lower. Each bolt was tipped with flame, burning her hotter as their kisses went on until she was melting and dripping with anticipation. Making pleading noises without conscious awareness of it.

The scoop of his hands under her backside surprised her, but her legs locked around his waist as he lifted her. She found herself nose to nose with him.

"Hold on." He looked as though he commanded armies, his face a mask of sharp angles as he carried her down the hall.

She clung across his shoulders, and buried her face in the masculine scents against his neck. She nuzzled his throat and lightly bit his earlobe, smiling when she made all the muscles in his body flex in reaction.

His hands tightened against her backside and she chuckled with feminine power, thrilling, then falling—

She gasped and let go to put out her hands, but he caught her with strong arms across her back, bending with her, coming with her and covering her as she landed gently on the mattress.

Barely any light had followed them into the room. They'd forgotten the baby monitor, but Lily was across the hall. Poppy would hear her—but dearly hoped she wouldn't.

She glanced toward the en suite.

"We'll get there," he murmured of the shower, propping himself over her on one elbow. "This is nice for now." His legs were tangled with hers, his hips heavy on hers.

With his free hand, he popped the first button on her top. *"Sí?"*

She smiled shyly, not sure what she was supposed to agree to. He could undress her if he wanted to, but this was the furthest thing from "nice." It was exhilarating and dangerous and consuming. It was everything she wanted.

And there was something awfully sweet about a man who wanted to seduce her when she was already there.

"You have to answer, *cariño.*" His fingers came up to comb tendrils of hair away from her face.

"Sí," she whispered.

"Perfecto." He stroked the backs of two fingers down her throat and finished opening her shirt, revealing her breasts in her demicups.

She tried to open his shirt, but, like the first time, had none of his skill. His buttons were small and tight. Impossible. He brought his hand up and brushed hers away then swept his hand in a sharp yank that tore off buttons and ripped holes.

She gasped. "You didn't have to do that!"

"I did," he assured her, catching her hand and bringing it to his hot chest. "I've waited a long time for your touch."

His words sent her heart into a spin. She greedily brushed aside the gaping edges of his shirt and claimed his taut skin. The texture of his chest hair played against her palms and his breath sucked in when she skimmed the heels of her hands across the tight points of his nipples.

He said something in Spanish that she didn't have the wherewithal to translate, but his hand slid across her waist, making her realize he had finished releasing her buttons and now took his time exploring all the flesh he had bared. He made a circle against her quivering belly, stroked his thumb across the bumps of her ribcage, then traced the zigzag stitching on the bottom of her bra.

She should have bought something better. Her underclothes were boring beige, purchased from a big box store. He didn't seem to mind. He drew circles on the soft cups.

There was no padding. She felt his touch almost as if she was naked. Her nipples stood up against the thin fabric, waiting for more. Begging for it.

Time stood still. His smile of pleasure was almost cruel as he teased her. She didn't realize she was furtively raking her thumbs across his nipples until his fierce gaze came up to hers and he said in a low growl, "Two can play that game, *preciosa.*"

With a casual flick of the front closure, her bra released and he brushed the cup aside. His nostrils flared as he took a moment to admire her blush-pink areoles and the turgid nipples atop them. Then he dipped his head, catching her nipple in his hot, damp mouth, devouring her.

She bit back a cry and arched, barely able to withstand the burn and rush of blood that made the tips unbearably tight and sensitive before he began to pull and tease and scrape with his teeth.

She bit her lip and thrust her fingers into his hair, but he didn't let up. He continued his delicious torture until she writhed against him, hips lifting in ancient signals of willingness.

He rose to kiss her mouth, drowning her in pure sensuality before he moved to her other breast, keeping his hand on the first, circling his thumb on the wet, taut button in a way that sent currents of desire straight through her. She grew wet with yearning. She was both embarrassed and becoming desperate, alternately trying to squeeze her thighs together and open them with invitation.

His legs were pinning hers, though, keeping her beneath him in a sensual vice where she couldn't escape the pleasure he was bestowing on her. She finally clasped the sides of his head and dragged his mouth up to hers again. She pushed her tongue between his lips, flagrant and uninhibited.

Take me, she begged with her kiss.

He groaned, shifted. Got his hand between them and released her jeans. He made another sound of deep satisfaction as he pushed his hand into her open fly, covering heat and damp cotton. His touch was wickedly skilled, rocking as he eased his touch deeper into the notch of her thighs, until she was lifting into the pressure of his palm, streaks of glorious pleasure arcing through her back. Only then did he slide a finger beneath the placket to brush her skin, leave her pulsing, then returning to soothe. Incite.

"I thought it was my imagination, the way you reacted like this," he said against her throat, deepening his caress in a way that was exquisitely satisfying, yet a profound tease.

"Rico." Growing mindless, she ran her hands over his chest and sides beneath his open shirt and across his back, arching to feel more of his naked skin with her bare breasts.

"Show me you weren't faking. Show me I can make it happen for you."

His trapped hand was making her wild. She moved with his touch, unable to resist the lure of the pleasure he offered. His mouth went back to her breasts and that was it. Seconds later she fell off the edge of the earth, but went soaring into the ether.

As cries of culmination escaped her parted

lips, he lifted his head and covered her mouth, kissing her with rapacious hunger that she returned with greed.

She gave up trying to open his belt and tried to worm her hands under it.

He was speaking Spanish again, swearing maybe. His hand caught her chin and he licked into her mouth as if he couldn't get enough of her. Then he made a pained noise as he lifted enough to jerk his own belt open and release his pants.

They moved in unison, pulling away to yank and divest and kick their pants off their legs. Naked, they rolled back into one another, near frantic.

This was how it had been that other time. There was no stopping this force. It was stronger than both of them.

And knowing he was as helpless to it as she was made it okay.

As he settled himself over her, however, she felt his tension. The care he took as he settled his hips low between her thighs and braced his weight on his elbows. She could feel his exertion of will over himself and by extension, her.

His whole body shook with the effort, but there was clarity behind the passion that glazed his eyes.

"Rico." She closed her eyes against that betrayal, wanting him to fall back into the miasma with her. She slid her touch between them, seeking the shape of him. So taut and smooth, damp on the tip, tight at the base.

His breathing grew ragged, telling her she was lacerating his control.

"Poppy." His voice reverberated from somewhere in his chest, ringing inside hers. "Open your eyes."

She didn't want him to read how anguished she was. How her soul was right there, seeking his as her body yearned for the impalement of his flesh. It was too much.

"Let me see you."

She opened her eyes and time slowed.

"Take me into you," he commanded, biting at her chin, using his powerful thighs to spread hers apart.

She guided the tip of him against her folds, parting, distantly thinking she ought to be more self-conscious, but she was only joyful. She was *aching*. She needed this slick motion of him against her sensitive button of nerves. She hummed with pleasure, growing wetter. Needier. She gloried in the pressure as he slowly forged into her, so hot as to burn her slick, welcoming flesh.

And sweet. Oh, the sweet, sweet easing of the ache as he invaded. The breadth of him was exactly as she remembered it. There was even a moment of distress when she thought he was more than her body could accept. Her fear eased within the next heartbeat as he settled and pulsed within her.

They were both quaking.

She thought he might have asked her if she was all right, but she only pulled him into a kiss. This moment was utterly perfect. She never wanted it to end.

But after a few drugging kisses, he began to move and she remembered now that pleasure was music on a scale, some notes sharper than others, but every single one a necessary part of the beautiful whole.

There was the smoothness of his skin across his shoulders, the power in them so delicious against the stroke of her palms. There was the friction of his waist against her inner thighs as her legs instinctively rose to hug him. The stretch of tendons at her inner thighs somehow added to the sweet tension that gripped her.

There was his mouth, dragging new, glorious sensations against her throat and jaw, then sucking her earlobe and making her scalp tighten before he kissed her, letting her taste the blatant sexuality in him. There was the silk of his hair grazing her cheek when he sucked a love bite against her neck. The moans they released were the chorus to their dance and the colors behind her closed eyes were matched only by the erotic sensations streaking through her whole body as he thrust and withdrew.

The sensations where they joined were particularly acute. No friction or tenderness, just shivering waves of joy that began lapping closer together, coiling tension within her until the intensity became unbearable.

"Rico." She writhed beneath him, fingernails digging into his buttocks, aching for more of him. Harder. *Deeper.*

"Only me." He held her face between his hands. Possessive, no question, but she thought she tasted wonder in the graze of his lips across hers. A strange reverence that sent quivers of joy through her whole being.

"Only you," she agreed. But she didn't think she could stand this level of tension. Trembles of arousal shivered over her, alarming in their intensity. "It's too much."

"Bear it," he said with a savage flash of his teeth. "Feel what we do to each other."

He moved in heavier strokes, her slippery heat gripping him instinctually, making the friction all the more acute and glorious. She gasped in breathless need as the universe opened with infinite possibility. Her hips rose to meet his and his shoulders shuddered with tension as he held back. Waited for her. Waited.

His eyes were black, his cheeks flushed. They were both coated in perspiration. She wanted to tear the flesh from his bones, she was at such a screaming pitch of arousal.

Then she tightened convulsively in the first notes of release. His control cracked. He moved faster, the bed squeaking beneath them. She didn't care about anything but the purposeful thrusting that was driving her so close to the edge she was ready to scream with agony. Anticipation. Craven demand for satisfaction. Her thighs clamped around his waist and her arms clung to his shoulders. She was ready to beg.

He made a feral noise and pushed his hand under her tailbone, tilted her hips and struck a fresh spear of sensation through her, throwing her soaring off the cliff, her climax so profound she opened her mouth in a soundless scream, gripped in the paroxysm of complete ecstasy.

While his own body clenched and shuddered over her. Within her. His eruption became an intimate complement to her own, extending her pulses of pleasure so they simply held each other tight, letting the convulsions, the clenches and twitches and fading pulses of aftershock wash over them again and again.

CHAPTER SEVEN

POPPY WOKE DAZED and tender and alone. She sat up, looking for the baby monitor without finding it. It was daylight. The clock said 9:10 a.m.

She looked at the pillow, but even though both of their suitcases were still standing near the foot of the bed, his pillow was undented.

After making love, they had dozed, caught their breath, then made love again. She had a vague recollection of him leaving after that. She hadn't been able to move or even ask where he was going, but apparently he hadn't come back.

Which put a hollow ache in her chest.

Waking alone felt like a terrible start to their marriage. She had thought his passion meant he wanted her. After soaring through the heavens most of the night, she was juddering back to earth, landing hard as she realized he might want her physically, but that was all.

She put on yesterday's clothes and scowled at her pale face in the mirror. Her hair stuck out like shocks of lightning and she couldn't even get a brush through it. She wanted to check on Lily before she showered, though. She grabbed the mass together in a fat ponytail and walked out in search.

A glance into the room where Lily had slept showed the single bed had also been slept in. Her heart panged at the evidence he hadn't had insomnia. He'd preferred to sleep apart from her. Were they to have a marriage like his parents? One based on "shared values"?

They shared two things—a child and passion. It might be enough to build on, but relationships were a two-way street. If he was going to put literal walls between them, they didn't stand a chance.

Telling herself this was only Day One and she needed to give this time, she continued to the lounge.

She found Rico on the sofa, reading his tablet and nursing a coffee. Lily was on a blanket nearby, working her way through a box of unfamiliar toys. She gave a scolding cry when Poppy appeared and held up her arms, demanding a cuddle where she rested her head on Poppy's shoulder while Poppy rubbed her back. Lily was a resilient little thing, but they both needed the reassurance of a hug after facing all these recent changes.

"Why didn't you wake me when she got up?" She hid behind their daughter, mouth muffled against Lily's hair while she kept her lashes lowered, too nervous of what she might see in his eyes to meet his gaze.

"I wanted to let you sleep." His voice rasped across her nerve endings, waking her to sensual memory without any effort at all. Maybe it was the words, the suggestion that he had worn her out—which he had.

"She's had toast and banana," he added. "The housekeeper is making us a proper breakfast. It should be ready shortly."

"I could have cooked."

"We pay her to do it."

Lily pointed at the toys and Poppy set her down to continue playing.

"Thank you." Poppy hugged herself. "I'm not used to anyone getting up with her. Gran could keep an eye on her if my back was turned, but Lily was getting too heavy and fast for her to do much else."

"A potential nanny is meeting us in Valencia. You can look forward to sleeping in every day, if you want to."

"I can look after my own daughter." Especially if she wasn't working. That part was bothering her. Her income had been piecemeal with a small, but reliable paycheck from working part-time at the bus depot and occasional top-ups with school portraits and the odd headshot or boudoir shoot. Now she was reliant on Rico. It was way too much like being a burden. Again.

"There will be many occasions when you'll have to be at my side without her. You'll want the consistency of a regular caregiver."

"What do you mean, 'many'?" She finally

looked at him, but he only raised his brows in mild surprise.

"Do you need a paper bag to breathe into? Why are you looking so shocked?"

"Because I thought you would go to work and maybe I'd find a job around your hours and we would eat dinner together, watch TV and go to bed like normal people."

He sipped his coffee. As he set it aside, he revealed a mouth curled into a mocking smile.

"This is my normal. Whether you work is entirely your choice. I know many power couples in which both spouses hold down high-profile positions."

Maybe not the bus depot, then.

"I also know many women, including my mother and Sorcha, who make a career of running a household, planning charity fundraisers and attending events in support of their husbands."

"How charmingly old-fashioned." She meant antiquated and patriarchal.

The deepening of his smirk told her he knew perfectly what she was saying.

"As I say, my normal. If you do intend to work, we'll definitely need a nanny. At least that much is settled."

Poppy wanted to stamp her foot in frustration. She couldn't go after him about doing his share on the childcare front, though. Not when he'd gotten up with Lily on his first morning with her, letting Poppy sleep in.

"I've booked a stylist to come by in an hour or so." His gaze went to her bare, unpolished toes and came back to her electrocuted hair.

Her hand went to the seam in her distressed jeans. "Why?"

"I'm introducing you and Lily to my parents this evening."

"I've met them," she reminded with an urge to laugh, because it was such a gross overstatement. She had stood behind Darna on three occasions without garnering even a glance as Darna had nodded understanding of the duquesa's orders. Rico's father had once held out a dirty glass as she walked by, not even looking at her, let alone thanking her for taking it.

"The press release will go out while we're there. I expect a few photographers will gather at the gate. You need to look the part."

"Paparazzi are going to want photos of *me*? Really?" She crossed one foot over the other and hugged herself. "How are your parents going to react to that?"

"By presenting a united front. That's why we're having dinner there."

"*Presenting* a united front," she repeated. "That tells me how sincerely they'll welcome me at their dining table, doesn't it? And then what?" She thought of all the gossip sites where she'd seen pictures of him with Faustina, then snapshots of his grim expression as he put her in the ground. "Rico, I can't do this," she realized with sudden panic. "I'm not prepared. You know I'm not."

"That's why I've called a stylist. You'll be fine."

To her horror, tears of frustration and yes, fear, pressed into her eyes, but the housekeeper came in and invited them to sit down to the breakfast she had prepared.

Poppy had to suck up her misgivings and let her new life unfold.

"You look beautiful," Rico said sincerely. "If you could drop the wide-eyed terror, you'd be flawless."

His attempt to lighten Poppy's mood fell flat.

Her stylist had understood perfectly the effect Rico wanted and had spent a good portion of the day achieving it.

Poppy wore a bronze slip with a lace overlay embroidered with copper roses. It was simple and feminine, sophisticated yet held a decidedly innocent flair. Her hair had been meticulously coaxed into tamer waves then gathered into a "casual" chignon suitable for a low-key dinner with family. Her makeup was all natural tones and her heels were a conservative height.

By the time he'd offered the jewelry he'd bought her, she'd looked like a dog that had been at the groomers so long she'd lost her will to live.

Now the fresh-faced nanny, who couldn't be more than a year over Poppy's age, suggested carrying Lily into the villa so their daughter wouldn't stain or snag Poppy's dress.

Rico agreed and Poppy shot him a glance of betrayal then fell into step beside him, mouth pouted.

Her angry dismay plucked at his conscience like a sour note on a string. He kept telling himself that she had already seen the workings of his family from an insider's perspective. None of this should be a surprise to her. And this was how it *was*. He couldn't pretend their life would be anything different. That would be a lie.

Even so, he sensed she'd put up a wall between them and it rankled. Which was hypocritical on his part because he'd taken steps to withdraw from her last night, after their lovemaking had left him in ruins.

What should have been a sensual celebration of a convenient marriage had become a conflagration that had turned him inside out. He had been right back to that interminable family dinner after his encounter with Poppy two years ago. Cesar and Sorcha had turned up—an engagement Rico had completely failed to recall had been scheduled. They'd eaten in polite silence while his mother had stiffly come to terms with Rico's wedding being off. She had already been floating the names of alternatives and a timeline for court-ship.

Rico had sat on the pin of a land mine, want-ing to rise from the table and go after Poppy. He hadn't seen a way in which he could even sustain an affair with her, though. As he'd eaten what might have been sawdust, facts had been reiterated about his father's pros-pects in the next election. The importance of certain alliances had been regurgitated.

Rico wasn't so shallow as to value money and appearances and power over all other things, but he understood how possessing those things allowed him and his family to live as comfortably as they did. All the ac-tions he took were about them, never only himself.

So, even though his engagement had been broken, even though he was sexually infatuated with his mother's maid, another bride would be slotted into place very quickly. The show must go on.

There had been some relief in living up to those expectations, too. As earth-shattering as his encounter with Poppy had been, he had instinctively recognized how dangerous that sort of passion was. How easily exposure to a woman who provoked such a deep response within him could dismantle him. Turn him against the best interests of his family and even impact him at a deeper level. A place even more vulnerable than the injuries of bruised ego and broken trust that his first wife had inflicted on him.

That premonition was playing out. His daughter had been the excuse, but the lure of Poppy had drawn him halfway around the world. He hadn't waited for tests to prove they should marry. He had accomplished it with haste and dragged her back here as quickly as he could.

Last night had proved to him they were still a volatile combination. Afterward, he'd felt so disarmed, so *satisfied* with having blown up his own life, he had had to leave her to put himself back together.

If Lily hadn't awakened a few hours later, he might very well have succumbed to temptation and crawled into bed with Poppy again.

He couldn't let her have that kind of power over him. That was what he kept telling himself. He had to keep control of himself or there would only be more scandal and disruption.

But he loathed that stiff look on her face.

It was too much like the ones on his parents' faces as they entered the small parlor where Faustina had once thrown down a vase like a gauntlet.

He ground his teeth, wishing at least Pia was here, chronically shy and uncomfortable as she might be. His sister was off studying snails or some other mollusk in the Galápagos Islands, however. Cesar had taken Sorcha and the boys to visit Sorcha's family in Ireland. There was nothing to soften this hard, flat evening for Poppy.

"My father, Javiero Montero y Salazar, Excelentísimo Senor Grandeza de España, and my mother, La Reina, the Duque and Duquesa of Castellón. You both remember Poppy." He wasn't trying to be facetious, but it came out that way.

His mother smiled faintly. "Welcome back."

Poppy was so pale he reached for her hand. It was ice-cold.

She delicately removed it from his hold and gave Lily's dress a small tug and drew the girl's finger from her mouth, smiling with tender pride. "This is Lily."

His parents both took a brief look at their granddaughter and nodded as if to say, *Yes, that is a baby.*

"A room has been prepared upstairs," Rico's mother said to the nanny, dismissing her and Lily in a blink.

The light in Poppy's eyes dimmed. It struck Rico like a kick in the gut.

This is who they *are*, he wanted to tell her.

There was no use wishing for anything different, but he could still hear the thread of hurt and rejection in her tone as she had told him about her parents never coming back for her.

He wanted to take her hand again, reassure her, but at his mother's invitation, she lowered to perch on an antique wing chair, hands folded demurely in her lap.

Champagne was brought in; congratulations were offered. Poppy's hand shook and he neatly slid a coaster under her glass before she set it on the end table.

His mother very tellingly said, "I imagine you're still settling in. We'll move into the dining room right away so the baby can have an early night."

This evening would *not* be a drawn-out affair. The rush was a slight, but Rico didn't want to subject Poppy to their company any longer than necessary so he didn't take issue with it.

The first course arrived and Poppy tried offering a friendly smile at the butler. It was countered with an impassive look that made her cheerful expression fall away. She blinked a few times.

The staff would talk to her when his parents weren't around, he wanted to tell her. This was how they were expected to act with guests and she shouldn't take it as a rejection.

His father cleared his throat.

Poppy glanced at him with apprehension. Rico briefly held his own breath, but his father only asked Rico about the progress he'd made on some alloy research.

Annoyed, Rico was forced to turn his attention to answering him, which left his mother to make conversation with Poppy.

"I'm told you enjoy photography, Poppy. How did your interest come about?"

Poppy shot him a look, but he hadn't provided that tidbit. This was also who his mother was. She would ferret out any item suitable for small talk that would avoid addressing more sensitive horrors like the fact Rico had messed with the maid, had an illegitimate child and brought them into the villa as "family."

Poppy spoke with nervous brevity. "When I was ten, my grandfather asked me to help him clean the basement. We came across his father's equipment. My great-grandfather was a freelance photographer for newspapers."

"What type of newspapers?" his mother asked sharply.

"Mother." Rico quit listening to his father and gave the women his full attention.

"The national ones," Poppy replied warily, sensing disapproval. "Sports, mostly. The odd royal visit or other big event. I was intrigued so my grandfather closed in a space and showed me how the development process worked."

"You should have shown me." Rico was ridiculously pleased to hear she shared the same spark of curiosity that had drawn him into chemical engineering.

"I haven't used it in years. We quickly realized the cost of chemicals and paper wasn't sustainable. I switched to digital photography."

"Metol or hydroquinone," Rico's father said

in one of his stark interjections, as though he'd retrieved a file from the dusty basement of his own mind. "Sodium carbonate and sodium sulfite for proper pH and delay of oxidation. Thiosulfate to fix it. None are particularly expensive, but there's no market for the premixed solutions. We got out of it years ago."

"Only niche artists are using them, I imagine," Poppy murmured.

"Speaking of art," his mother said with an adept pivot from boring science. "I'm attending an opening in Paris next month. I imagine you'll be decorating a house very soon. What sort of pieces might you be looking for?"

Poppy looked as though a bus was bearing down on her.

"It's early days, Mother," Rico cut in. "We'll talk more about that another time."

At this point he was only looking as far as getting through this evening.

The meal passed in a blur of racking her brains for the names of Canadian politicians who might have said something brilliant or stupid lately and trying to look as if she knew how to eat quail in gazpacho. Poppy was infinitely relieved when they left and went to Rico's Valencian penthouse.

This wasn't a family property. It was his own home, purchased after Faustina had died. It was luxurious and in a prime location with a pool and a view, but it was a surprisingly generic space, tastefully decorated in masculine tones yet completely without any stamp of his personality.

She dismissed the nanny, put Lily to bed herself, then moved into the bedroom to kick off her heels and sigh with exhaustion.

Rico came in with a nightcap for each of them.

She immediately grew nervous. It had been a long, trying day, one that had started out with a rebuff when she'd woken alone. That sense of foreboding had grown worse as his stylist had spent hours turning her into some kind of show pony.

She suspected she had disappointed anyway. As he set down his own drink and loosened his tie, she had a sick, about-to-be-fired feeling in her stomach, much like the one she'd had when she'd lost her first babysitting job after accidentally letting the hamster out of its cage.

"Well?" she prompted, trying to face the coming judgment head-on.

"I thought it went well."

She strangled on a laugh. "Are you kidding? I've never spent a more horrendous two hours and twenty-three minutes in my life."

"You were there, then." He shrugged out of his jacket.

"Don't make jokes, Rico." She stared at him, but he wasn't laughing. Uncertain, she asked, "Was that really a normal dinner for you? The way it's been your whole life?" She had thought her own mother awful for calling in lame efforts at nurturing with insincere apologies from afar. His parents had displayed zero remorse as they had openly dismissed his newfound daughter.

"Don't be ridiculous," he said with scathing sarcasm. "I didn't sit at that table until I was twelve. Children are invited to the dining room when they know how to eat quietly and speak only when spoken to."

She thought of the way Lily squealed and slapped her tray and wore more food than she ate. But even Gran with her old-fashioned ideals about child-rearing had always insisted that dinner was a time for the whole family to come together.

"Why are they *like* that?"

He stripped his tie and threw it away with a sigh. "My father is a scientific genius. He only speaks logic and rational debate. Emotion has no effect on him. It's one of the reasons he makes a genuinely good politician. He reads and considers policy on its own merit, not worrying about his popularity or future prospects. Mother was born with a title, but no money. She had to marry it and prove she was worth the investment. Having brought herself up this far, she refuses to backslide. And, after thirty-five years of my father's lack of sentiment, she's abandoned any herself."

"That sounds so empty. Is she happy?"

"They set out with specific goals and achieved them. They are content, which is the standard to which we've been taught to aspire."

She searched his expression. "And you're *content* with that?"

"Why wouldn't I be? My life is extremely comfortable." He peeled off his shirt, revealing his gorgeous chest and tight abs.

She swallowed and turned away, annoyed with herself for reacting so promptly to the sight of him.

"Is that why you agreed to an arranged marriage the first time? To maintain the status quo?"

"Yes. I was expected to do my part in preserving the life we all enjoy." His voice was suddenly right behind her, surprising her into lifting her gaze to the mirror.

He lightly smoothed his hand across her shoulders, grazing an absent caress against her nape as he ensured no tendrils of hair would catch as he unzipped her.

"How angry are they that Lily and I ruined everything?" She braced herself as she held his gaze. "Be honest. I need to know."

"They don't get angry." He sounded mild, but she thought she caught a flicker of something in his stoic expression.

"What about you? You were angry when you showed up at my door."

"And I wound up telling you something I had sworn to take to my grave. Heightened emotions don't help any situation."

"What does that mean?" With a niggling premonition, she began unpinning her hair, not wanting to remove the gaping dress and be naked when she was beginning to feel defenseless. "I want to fit in, Rico. I want to be a team player and know what to say about decor and houses and all those different people she was talking about. But along with not being prepared to live at this level of wealth, I'm wired for emotion. Don't expect me never to get angry. Or to stop feeling."

His cheek ticked and she could hear the

thoughts behind that stiff mask. *Don't expect me to start.*

Which made her angry. Furious that she'd spent every minute since he'd shown up on her doorstep having her emotions bombarded until they were right there, under the thin surface of her skin, tender and raw, while he had somehow used tonight's endurance event of a dinner to shore up his shields so he was more withdrawn than ever.

"That's what you want, though, isn't it?" she realized, appalled to see her shimmering nascent hopes for deeper intimacy disappearing faster than she could conjure them. "You want me to learn not to care. To feel nothing. Certainly I shouldn't aspire to happiness, should I?"

"Happiness is achieved by keeping your expectations realistic. That's a proven fact."

It was such a cynical thing to say, it physically hurt her to hear it.

"What about desire?" In a small stab at getting through to him, she let the dress fall off her arms. She stepped out of it before tossing it onto the foot of the bed. "Do you want me to quit feeling *that*?"

"That's physical." He let his gaze rake slowly down her pale form from shoulder to thighs, jaw hardening along with his voice. "And you're starting a fight for no reason."

"I'm sorry you feel that way," she said facetiously. "I'm going to shower. Would you like to join me? Yesterday it was one of your many fantasies, but maybe you *feel* different today."

His eye ticked and she knew he was sorry he had ever told her that. Did she feel guilty for using it? Not one bit.

She slid her panties down and left them on the floor.

It was a bold move, one far beyond her experience level. If he left her to shower alone, she would probably drown herself in there, but she desperately wanted to prove to both of them that she had some kind of effect on him. Some means of reaching through that armor of his.

She moved into the bathroom and stepped

into the marble-tiled stall, bigger than the porch on Gran's bungalow.

He came into the bathroom as the steam began to gather around her. He dimmed the light so the gilded space became golden and moody and he stripped off his pants.

She watched him, reacting with an internal clench when she saw he was aroused.

When he came into the shower, she lost some of her moxie and turned her face into the rain of warm water from the sunflower head above her.

His cool hands settled on her hips and his thumbs dug lightly into the tops of her butt cheeks. "You have a gorgeous ass."

"Even with the dimples?" Her heartbeat was unsteady.

"Especially with." He took hold of the wet mass of her hair, holding her head tipped back while he scraped his teeth against the side of her neck. "I will always accept this invitation, Poppy. But you had better know what you're inviting."

She gasped. The sensations he was causing

were cataclysmic. All her senses came alive. He settled his cool body against her back, his chest hair lightly brushing before the warm water sealed them together. His hard shaft pressed into the small of her back and her buttocks tightened in excited reaction. Her breasts grew heavy, her loins tingled. The humid air became too heavy to breathe and her bones melted like wax in the sun.

Blindly she shot a hand out to the slick wall and wound up leaning both hands there while her hips instinctively tipped with invitation.

"What are you trying to prove?" he growled, slapping one hand beside her own on the wall.

Nothing. She was reacting, pure and simple.

He briefly covered her like any male mounting his mate and his teeth sank lightly against her nape again. His free hand splayed across her abdomen, then roamed her wet skin to cup her breast.

In a sudden move, he pulled her upright and spun her so the world tilted around her. She found the hard tiles against her shoulders. His knees nudged between hers and his thighs pinned hers. He bracketed her head between his forearms and touched his nose to hers before he claimed the kiss she was starving for.

He held nothing back, wet mouth sliding across hers with carnal greed, slaking her thirst after this arid day. She flowered. She opened and ran with dewy nectar. She unfurled her arms around him and twined them across his back, lifted her knee up to his hip and invited him into her center. Rocked and tried to make him lose control the way she continued to abandon hers.

"Let's talk about your fantasies, hmm?" His hands caught her wrists and pinned them beside her head while his tongue slithered down her neck and licked into the hollow at the base of her throat. "What do you want?"

He drew back slightly and gazed down on her with unabashed hunger.

"Rico." She turned her wrist in his grasp and shifted with self-consciousness. Her nipples stood up with blatant, stinging arousal. She brought her foot back down to the floor, but his feet were still between hers.

"Did you ever touch yourself and imagine it was me?" He dropped one hand and drew his fingertip through her swollen folds, looking down again as he languidly caressed her. "Did you want to *feel* my hand here?"

She was immediately disoriented, glad for the hard wall at her back as she rose into his touch and draped her arm across his shoulders, seeking balance.

"Tell me," he commanded between kisses. "Tell me or I'll stop."

"Yes," she gasped.

He rewarded her by bending to suck one nipple, then the other, driving further spikes of pleasure into that place he continued to tease. A keening noise sounded and she realized it was her, unable to express her agonizing climb of desire in any other way.

Now he was on his knees, licking at her. Splaying her and gently probing and circling and driving her to the brink of madness. She realized distantly that she had her hands fisted in his wet hair, that she had completely abandoned herself to him. To the exquisite pleasure he relentlessly inflicted upon her. Within moments, cries of ecstasy tore from her throat, filling the steamy, hollow chamber.

He ran his mouth all over her thighs and stomach, soft bites that claimed his right to do so as she stood there weakly, heart palpitating, breath still splintered.

He stood and snapped the water off, staring at her while she leaned helpless and overwhelmed. Outdone.

Meeting his gaze was like looking into the sun, painful in its intensity. Painful in how blind and exposed she felt, but she couldn't look away. Couldn't pretend he hadn't peeled her down to her core until she was utterly at his mercy.

While he remained visibly aroused, but in complete control.

"The way we make each other feel is a hell of a lot more than many couples have. Recognize that. Be satisfied with it."

She wasn't and never would be.

But when he held out a hand, she let him

balance her as she stepped out onto the mat. He dried her off and took her to his bed, where he satisfied her again and again and again.

CHAPTER EIGHT

RICO WOKE IN the guest bed he'd been using all week and listened, thinking Lily must be stirring. He ought to be sleeping more heavily considering the quantity and quality of sex he was enjoying, but his radar remained alert to the other occupants of his penthouse.

He listened, thought he must be imagining things, started to drift off then heard the burble of a video chat being connected. The volume lowered.

He rose, already wearing boxers in case he had to go to Lily. His door was cracked and it swung open silently, allowing him to hear Poppy's hushed voice reassuring her grandmother.

"No, everything's fine. I couldn't sleep and thought this would be a good chance to chat without a baby crawling all over me. How are you settling in?"

"Same as I told you yesterday," her grandmother said wryly. "You're the one with the gadabout life. What have you been up to?"

He stood and listened to Poppy relay that the nanny had taken Lily for a walk today while she had pored over properties with a real estate agent. He'd been going in to work each day, but taking her out at night. She mentioned this evening's cocktail party where he had introduced her to some of his top executives and their wives.

She made it sound as though she had had the time of her life when she'd actually been petrified and miserable, not that she'd been obvious about it. He knew how she behaved when she was comfortable, though. She laughed with Lily and traded wry remarks with her grandmother.

That woman was making fewer and fewer appearances when she was with him, however, which was beginning to niggle at him. He glimpsed her when they made love. She held nothing back in bed, but tonight she had disappeared quickly after they had wrung untold pleasure from each other. She had rolled away and her voice had pulled him from his postcoital doze.

"Will you check on Lily as you go?"

"Of course." He had told himself he was glad she'd kept him from falling asleep beside her. His will to leave her each night grew fainter and fainter, but staying seemed the even weaker action. He wasn't Lily, needing his cuddle bear clutched in his arm in order to drift off.

He wasn't sure what he had expected from this marriage. When contemplating his first to Faustina, he had anticipated following his parents' example. Like his siblings, he had been raised to keep his emotions firmly within a four-point-five and a four-point-seven. Not a sociopath, but only a few scant notches above one. He had never been a man of grand passions anyway and had been comfortable with the idea of a businesslike partnership with his spouse.

That certainly hadn't worked out. Given the betrayal and drama he'd suffered at Faustina's hands, he had wanted this marriage to conform to that original ideal.

It didn't. Poppy didn't. He kept telling himself she would get used to this life, but seeing her natural exuberance dim by the day was eating at him. He didn't know what to do about it, though. This was their reality.

"Dinner will be served soon. I have to start making my way or it will be cold by the time I arrive," Eleanor said with a papery chuckle.

"Okay. I love you. I miss you." She ended the call, but didn't rise.

He was growing cold standing there, but didn't go back to bed. He could see her shoulders over the back of the sofa. They rose slightly as she sighed deeply. Her breath caught with a jag. She sniffed.

A terrible swoop of alarm unbalanced him. The embarrassed moment of walking in on something personal struck, yet he couldn't turn away and leave her to it.

As her shoulders began to shake and she

ducked her head into her hands, beginning to weep in earnest, a rush of something indefinable came over him. A sharp, shimmering, deeply uncomfortable *ache* gripped him. It was so excruciating, it made him want to close himself in the guest room and wait for it to pass.

But he couldn't turn his back on her while she was like that. A far stronger compulsion pushed him down the hall toward her.

"Poppy." Her name scratched behind his breastbone. At some level he understood he was responsible for this misery she was exhibiting. He had some scattered thoughts of all that he was providing her, but he knew she didn't care about those things. She was a complex, emotional creature and it struck him how completely ill-equipped he was to handle that.

She lifted a face tracked with silver and made an anguished noise, clearly mortified that he was seeing her this way. Again he thought to give her privacy, but he couldn't let her suffer alone. This was his fault. That much he understood and it weighed very heavily on him.

"Come." He gathered her up, the silk of her pajamas cool against his naked chest.

"I don't want to make love, Rico. I want to go *h-home*." The break in her voice rent another hole in him.

"Shh." He carried her to the bed where he'd left her a few hours before and crawled in with her to warm both of them. He told himself that was what this was, even though the feel of her against him had the effect of pressing a cut together. It didn't fix it, but it eased some of the pain. Slowed the bleeding and calmed the distress. "It's okay," he murmured.

"No, it's not." Her words were angry, despairing sobs. "I'm so homesick I hurt all the time. At least the last time I was stuck here, I made friends, but no one will talk to me."

"Who's refusing to speak to you?" he asked with sharp concern.

"*Everyone.* The staff. They only ask me if I want something, never joke or make me feel like they like me. They're only being polite because you pay them to be."

"That's not true." He suddenly glimpsed how isolated she must be in her new position and cursed himself for not recognizing it would be so acute.

"I have nothing in common with *your* friends. They talk too fast for me to even understand them. You're Lily's father and I want her to know you, Rico. I know I have to stay here for her sake, but why does the nanny get to take her for a walk while I have to go to stupid parties? I hate it here. I hate it so much."

"Shh," he soothed, closing his hand around the tight fist on his chest and kissing her hard knuckles. "This is going to be an adjustment for all of us."

"How is this an adjustment for *you*? You're completely unaffected! I can't do this, Rico. I *can't*."

His neck was wet and her hair stuck to the tear tracks, keeping that fissure in him stinging. He rubbed her back, trying to calm her while her desolation shredded his ability to remain detached.

There are some realities that are not worth crying about, he had told Mateo a few weeks ago. He'd been taught to believe no one would care, but he *did* care. Not the generic regard of one human for another, but a deeper, more frightening feeling he didn't know how to process.

Everything in him warned that he should distance himself, but he couldn't ignore her pain.

He knew what he had to do. It would cost him, but he would do it. This anguish of hers was more than he could bear.

Poppy woke from the dense fog of a deep sleep to hear Rico's morning voice rasping on the baby monitor.

"We'll let Mama sleep this morning."

The transmission clicked off, but as Poppy rolled onto her back and straightened her limbs, she discovered the warm patch beside her on the bed.

He had stayed the night? She was chagrined that he'd caught her in the middle of a pity party, but she hadn't been able to hold it in any longer. She had tried, honestly tried not to care about all of those things.

She did care, though. She was lonely and out of her depth. Her only friend was the daughter she had to share with a nanny who adored her, but whom Poppy was growing to resent by the day.

She threw her arm over her eyes, trying not to spiral back into melancholy. They had appointments to view properties today, she recalled. She could hardly wait to have a bigger house to get lost in, and more staff to treat her like some kind of visiting foreign official.

A few hours later, she was beside Rico as he drove a shiny new SUV up the coast. Poppy had understood the property agent would be driving them to view potential homes, but she didn't complain. It felt nice to be just the three of them for a change.

"You should have told me to bring my camera," she murmured, quite sure she would have a kink in her neck from swiveling her attention between the sunny coastal beaches and the craggy hillocks interspersed with picturesque ancient villages. "I'm used to staring at wheat and sunflower fields on long drives."

"Think about what sort of space you want for your studio as we look at potential homes. I'm sure a darkroom could be built into just about any corner of a house, but give some thought to how that will fit with our day-to-day living."

"A darkroom! I told you, that's expensive." She wouldn't mind a studio, though.

"As it turns out, I happen to have money. If that's where your interest lies, pursue it." He turned into a private road that lacked a for sale sign and wound through a vineyard.

"There's no money in photography." Not the sort his level of society expected a woman to make if she was going to pursue a career over homemaking.

"I don't expect you to make money. Do it for yourself. Be an artist."

"You're going to be my patron? Don't pander to me just because I acted like Lily last night." She spoke to the window to hide her embarrassment.

"I'm not. I want you to be happy."

That swung her around because no, he didn't. He had specifically told her to settle.

He might have recalled that conversation, too. His expression grew stiff as he braked and threw the vehicle into Park.

Poppy glanced around. "I don't see the agent."

"It's not for sale. This is Cesar and Sorcha's home."

"Why didn't you tell me we were meeting them today?" She glanced down at the pantsuit she'd put on hoping to look the part of a rich man's wife viewing villas as if she knew what such a man needed.

"You look perfect." He stepped out. "They don't know we're coming so they'll be equally casual."

"Why don't they know we're coming?" she asked as he came around while she was opening the back door to get Lily.

"You're supposed to wait for me to come around and open your door for you," he chided.

"I know how to open my own car door. I also know how to look after my own daughter." She brushed him away from trying to reach in, then grunted as she released Lily and took her weight, dragging her out. "What I don't know is how I'm supposed to behave when you drop me on relatives who don't know I'm coming."

Lily squinted as Poppy drew her from the car and buried her face in Poppy's neck.

"I'll keep her," Poppy murmured as Rico tried to take her. It was pathetic to hide behind her daughter, but she needed Lily's sturdy warmth to bolster her.

A maid let them in and the view took her breath as they moved from the foyer to a front room where huge picture windows overlooked the Mediterranean.

"Tío!" A young boy of about four ran in wearing red trunks and nothing else.

Rico picked him up. "You remember Enrique? Cesar's eldest?" he asked Poppy.

"You've grown," she murmured. *"Bon dia,"* she added in the small amount of Valencian dialect she knew the family used among themselves.

"Say hello to Poppy and Lily," Rico prompted him.

"Hola. ¿Cómo estás?" Enrique asked with a confidence beyond his years.

Rico gave Enrique's backside a pat. "You're wet. How are you swimming? It's too early in the year."

"I got in to here." Enrique touched his belly button.

"And now you're eating your lunch," Cesar said, strolling in wearing crisp linen pants and a shirt he was buttoning. He nodded to send Enrique back outside.

This was the most relaxed Poppy had ever seen Cesar, but he still projected a chilly formality not unlike the duque and duquesa. In fact, he greeted his brother with a look that bordered on hostile.

"You've lost your drop-in privileges with my family." It was a very civil, *Get the hell out.*

Because of her and Lily? Because they were a stain on the family name?

With a muted noise of distress, Poppy closed her arms protectively around Lily and looked to the door.

Rico glanced at her with concern then scowled at his brother. "Now you've gone and hurt *my* wife's feelings."

Cesar frowned at her. His gaze dropped to Lily and his frown eased.

"Whose feelings?" Sorcha came up behind her husband. She was blond and effortlessly beautiful in a summer dress with a forget-me-not print. Daywear diamonds sparkled in her ears.

"Poppy." Her surprise warmed into a welcoming smile that sent the first trickles of relief through Poppy's defensively stiff limbs. "And here's Lily." Sorcha came right up to them and gave Lily's elbow a tickle. She tilted her head to meet the gaze Lily shyly kept tucked into Poppy's neck.

"Will you come see me? Let me introduce you to your cousins?" Sorcha held out her hands. "They'll share their lunch with you. Are you hungry?"

Lily went to her. Who could resist the promise of food and the warm lilt of an Irish accent?

"Thank you, darling. That's quite a compliment." Sorcha cuddled her close, then glanced at Rico. Her tone dropped to permafrost. "*You* can wait in the car."

"I deserve that," Rico said with tense sincerity. "I regret the hurt I caused you. I wouldn't interrupt your weekend, but Poppy needs you, Sorcha. Will you help her? If not for me, then for her sake and Lily's? Please? I know how you feel about family."

"That's below the belt!" Sorcha tucked her chin, looked as though she wanted to punish him further, then gave a little sigh. "Since you've brought me this *very* precious gift—" She snuggled Lily more securely onto her hip. "I will forgive you. *This one time.*" She smiled at Poppy without reserve. "And of course I'll help you any way I can. I would have called you later this week." Another dark look toward Rico. "I didn't want to wait until our gala next month. I'm so glad you're here. Come join us."

"What did you do?" Poppy hissed at Rico as he fell into step beside her.

"Said something that doesn't bear repeating." To her surprise, he took her hand and wove their fingers together, giving her a little squeeze. "But Sorcha knows what you're up against. Let her be your guide."

It struck her that this had been hard for him. She doubted it was in his nature to ask for help any more than it was in hers. He and Cesar were obviously on rocky ground, but he had invaded their family time for her sake.

"Please tell Chef we're four adults and three children for lunch now," Sorcha said easily to the hovering butler.

"Champagne," Cesar added, holding Sorcha's chair as she lowered with Lily and kept her in her lap. "Boys, this is your cousin, Lily. Can you say hello and welcome her and Auntie Poppy to the family?"

Enrique began to giggle. He pointed his fork at Cesar. "That's Papi."

Poppy smiled. "Maybe you'll have to call this one Tío Mama now." She thumbed toward Rico as he helped her with her own chair.

Enrique nearly tumbled out of his, laughing at the absurdity as he repeated, "Tío Mama."

Poppy bit her lip with remorse, suspecting she'd released a genie that wouldn't go easily back into its bottle. She called on one of Gramps's favorite tricks for getting through to a child who had a case of the sillies. She leaned over and spoke very softly so Enrique would have to quiet to hear her.

"My grandfather used to tell me it was okay to tease your family with a funny name when you were alone, but you have to remember to be respectful when you're with others. Will you be able to do that?"

Enrique nodded and clamped his smile over his fork, eyes full of mischief as he looked at Rico.

"Sorry," Poppy mouthed as she caught Sorcha's amused glance. "You have a very beautiful home," she added, glancing at the placid pool and the profusion of spring blooms surrounding it.

"Thank you. We're extremely happy here." Sorcha looked to her husband for confirmation, but her smile reflected more than happiness. Even two years ago it had been obvious to Poppy these two were deeply in love.

While Rico wore his customarily circumspect expression.

"I want one of those," Cesar informed Sorcha with smoky warning, nodding at Lily where she sat contentedly in Sorcha's lap, fist clenched around a spear of juicy peach.

"Let's keep this one." Sorcha pressed her smile to the top of Lily's head. "She's exactly what we've been thinking of."

"We should probably try making our own before we resort to stealing."

"Picky, picky. But if you insist, I'll have my people talk to your people. Schedule a one-on-one for further discussion."

"Really?" Rico drawled of the flirty banter. "In front of the children?"

"They've walked in on worse," Cesar muttered, rising as the butler arrived with the champagne. "Learn to lock doors," he advised while Sorcha looked to the sky.

The lunch passed with easy chatter and the wiping of sticky fingers.

"I'm so glad Rico brought you today," Sorcha said later, after a travel cot had been found for Lily and she'd been put down for her afternoon nap while the men took the boys into the vineyard. Sorcha sobered. "I'm very glad he went looking for you. Are you angry with me?"

"For telling him? No." Poppy crossed her arms. "I'd been thinking about doing it. Things were complicated at home so I put it off, but it's all worked out." For Gran and Lily. Her? Not so much.

"I'm sorry for interfering. I know how hard that decision can be, but I couldn't let him miss out on Lily. He shut right down after Faustina. My heart broke clean in half for him. I'm so happy to see the way he's taken to her."

Poppy nodded dumbly, shielding her gaze with a glance toward the floor so Sorcha couldn't read the bigger story in her eyes.

"He wants to be a good father. I was afraid of... Well, nothing, I guess," Poppy admitted ruefully. When it came to Rico's feelings for Lily, she had every confidence their bond would only continue to grow.

"But?" Sorcha prompted.

"It's hard." Her throat thickened and she felt tears pressing behind her eyes. "This is all really hard. Rico and I don't have what you and Cesar did. The years of familiarity and caring."

Sorcha choked on a laugh. "Do I make it look like it was easy for us to get where we are? That is quite a compliment and good on me for selling that image, but no. I assure you that what we have was achieved through blood, sweat and tears. Years of loving my boss, if you want the truth. Which is how and why Enrique came about," she added dryly. "But like the rest of his family, Cesar had kicked his heart under the sofa and forgotten about it. So there will definitely be some heavy lifting required to find Rico's. I'm sorry to tell you that." Sorcha sobered. "But I think it's understandable, given what he's been through."

Sorcha thought she knew what Rico had been through, but he wasn't nursing a broken heart over a lost baby. That was what made this so hard. This wasn't a matter of mending his heart. Or finding it. It was a matter of him wanting to give it to her. And he didn't.

But she only nodded again, protecting the secret Rico had entrusted to her.

"It will all be worth it, Poppy. I promise you," Sorcha said with a squeeze of her arm. "In the meantime, you have me. I'm happy to help you navigate this new world. When I was in your position, I needed help, too. One of these days we'll go shopping with my friend Octavia. She really does know how to make all of this look easy. For now, let's go to my closet. I'll show you what is absolutely essential. Try not to faint."

* * *

Poppy could feel Rico's heart slowing to lazy slams beneath her breast. Her sweating body was splayed bonelessly across him. She knew she ought to move, but he stroked his hand down her spine and traced a circle on her lower back, making her shiver. She clenched around him in a final aftershock of ecstasy.

He turned his head, brushing his lips against her temple in what she took as a signal to move. As she started to pry herself off him, however, his arms closed more firmly around her.

"You can stay right here all night," he murmured lazily.

"Don't you want to go to the guest room?"

His arms dropped way from her. She rolled off him.

"Do you want me to?" All the indolent warmth disappeared from his tone.

"No." Her voice was barely audible. "But why are you staying? Because you feel sorry for me?"

"No. Why would you think that?"

"You slept with me last night because I was crying."

"I came to bed with you because you were crying. I stayed because I wanted to."

"You didn't want to those other nights?"

A sigh.

"Rico, I keep telling you I've never done this before. This might be how you normally conduct a sexual relationship, but it's not the way I thought marriage was supposed to be."

He bit off a laugh. "This isn't normal. That is the problem, Poppy." He sighed and repeated more somberly, "That is the problem."

Even she, with her limited experience, understood that their passion was exceptional. She had climaxed three times before he'd clasped hard hands to her hips and bucked beneath her, releasing with a jagged cry. She imagined she would have fingerprint bruises under her skin and perversely enjoyed having such an erotic reminder linger for days.

Sex was the easy part. Talking to him, catching him alone and digging up the courage to speak her mind and face difficult answers was the hard part. But she made herself do it.

"Is that why you haven't wanted to sleep with me? Too much sex? Am I being too demanding?"

He blew out a breath that was amused yet exasperated. "No. Although I fear for our lives on a nightly basis."

"Please don't make jokes, Rico. I need to understand. You're the one who said I should keep my expectations realistic. Tell me what realistic looks like because I don't *know*."

"I don't know, either," he admitted after a moment. "That's why I'm not processing this any better than you are. I thought our first time was an anomaly. It wasn't. It's shocking to me how powerfully we affect each other. It doesn't matter that you just spent an hour wringing me out. I want you again. *This isn't normal.*"

"I don't like it, either! I hate that you can snap your fingers and I fall onto my back."

He threw his arm over his eyes and released a ragged, self-deprecating laugh. "I'm the one who was on his back tonight, *corazón.* In case you hadn't noticed."

"It's not very comforting to hear that when you're clearly annoyed by it. Why does it bother you so much that we react this strongly?"

Another silence where she thought he might ignore her question. Finally he admitted, "Passion is dangerous. You know that Cesar was in a car crash some years ago?"

"I only know what's online about it."

"Mmm. Well, it happened after he slept with Sorcha. Directly after. I'd always been aware he had a physical infatuation with her. He didn't give in to base urges any more than I ever thought I would, but that day he did. And he decided the passion they shared was worth blowing up his life for. Mother was pushing him toward an arranged marriage. He went to Diega and told her he wouldn't be asking her to marry him. We don't know if he was overwrought or what, but he skidded off the road after he left her and nearly died."

Part of her panged with empathy. For all

his habitual detachment and his recent disagreement with Cesar, Rico was as close to his brother as he was capable of being with anyone. It must have been a terribly worrisome time for him.

But what she also heard was that he really did think the passion between them posed a mortal danger—which equally told her he would hold her at arm's length because of it.

"It's not like I'm doing this on purpose, you know." She rolled away. "I'm a victim, too."

"I know." He followed her, dragging her into the spoon of his body. His voice tickled hotly through her hair. "I'm realizing that uncontrollable passion isn't only a crazed act in a quiet solarium. It's a hunger that refuses to be ignored. I'm not a dependent person, Poppy. I don't like being unable to suppress a craving that isn't a *need*. But I don't see the sense in hurting you, making your assimilation here more difficult because I'm displeased with myself."

It was hardly a declaration of love, but he

didn't want to hurt her. It was something. She relaxed deeper into the bend of his body.

"You *are* trying to kill me," he accused, aroused flesh pressed to her backside.

She rolled to face him, stretching against him in a full-body caress.

"Maybe this is our normal."

"Maybe it is. Let's hope we survive it."

Over the next few weeks, Poppy tried to think of this new life as something she could do, rather than something that was being done *to* her. It helped to take the wheel, even if she wasn't sure where she was going. She began reviewing the week's menu with the housekeeper and making additions to the shopping list. She toured several properties and told Rico why she felt some of them wouldn't suit—one had a distinct perfume in the air from the fertilized fields next door, another had rooms that were very closed off from one another.

Rico was dead set on getting a vineyard again and wanted a pool. Poppy mentioned she'd prefer to be close to Sorcha and Lily's new cousins, to which he said, "Of course. That's the area I'd prefer as well."

She even sat down with the nanny and cleared the air. Poppy admitted this was all new to her and she sometimes felt threatened. Ingrid confessed to feeling she wasn't working hard enough and that's why she kept stepping up, trying to take Lily off her hands. By the time they finished their coffee and cake, they'd worked out the fine points of a long-term contract, both of them relaxed and smiling.

Rico continued dragging her to dinners and networking events, but they went more smoothly after she began taking Sorcha's advice and asking the other wives for recommendations on things like shoe boutiques and hair stylists. Their responses went in one ear and out the other, but at least they seemed to warm to her.

"Let me know when you need an interior designer," one said at one point.

"We have to find a house first. That's proving a challenge," Poppy admitted with genuine frustration.

Twenty minutes of sharing her wish list later, the woman offered a lead on a property that was farther up the coast from Cesar's villa. It wasn't officially on the market, but rumor had it the family needed the money and would accept the right offer.

Rico made a few discreet inquiries and they viewed it the next day.

"I asked Mother if she knew anything about it. She said to be careful when we open the closets," Rico told her as they stepped from the car.

"Skeletons?" Poppy asked, but her smile wasn't only amusement. Despite the clear signs of age and neglect, a covetous joy rang through her as she took in the stone house, instantly falling in love with the tiled roof and cobbled walkway and darling gated courtyard where she imagined Lily safely playing for hours.

Arches down the side formed a breezeway that wrapped around both levels then overlooked the pool—which needed repair and filling—but it offered a view of the Med that rivaled Cesar and Sorcha's.

Inside, the rooms were desperate for updating. Rico went a step further and said, "This floor plan should be completely reconfigured."

"When are they moving out?" she asked, looking at the furniture draped in sheets.

"They've already taken what they want. We would buy it as is. Mother will know which collectors to call to get rid of most of this."

The scope of the project was enormous, but Poppy was strangely undaunted. In fact, as she discovered a spiral staircase, she excitedly scooted up it. The small rooftop patio looked in every direction for miles and doubled as a sheltered place for intimate dining, utterly charming her.

"We could build out this direction," Rico said, firmly holding on to Lily as he leaned to see off the side. "Perhaps put a guest cottage at the edge of the orange grove."

There were other fruit trees along with a

flower garden and a plot off the kitchen for a small vegetable garden, something Poppy's grandparents had always had when she'd been young. It became too much for all of them in later years, but the idea of Lily eating fresh strawberries gave Poppy such a sense of nostalgia and homecoming, she had to swallow a cry of excitement.

"Everything is pollinated by the bee hives in the lower corner," Rico informed her, referring to some notes on his phone. "Apparently we would have our own honey."

Poppy blinked. "Why do I love the idea of keeping bees?"

"I don't know, but I'm intrigued, too."

As they walked out a lower door to view the hives, Rico nodded meaningfully at an exterior door. "Wine cellar."

She knew what he was driving at and shook her head, not wanting to get her hopes up. It was too perfect already. "You'd need it for wine, wouldn't you?"

They entered a big, dim room filled with nearly empty racks. While he glanced at the labels on the handful of bottles left behind, she explored the rear of the cellar, discovering a narrow, windowless room with a low ceiling. A few shelves held empty glass canning jars, suggesting it was a root cellar. A bare bulb was the only light.

Poppy was overwhelmed by what seemed like her birthday, Christmas and every other wish-making day come true. She began arranging her future darkroom. The tubs would go there, the enlarger there. She might cry, she wanted this so badly.

"Am I wrong or is this everything we want?" Rico was carrying Lily and followed Poppy into the narrow room.

This was everything she could ever wish for herself and her daughter. The only thing she could want after this was her husband's heart.

Her own took an unsteady tumble as she realized how deeply she was yearning for that when every other part of their marriage was slotting into place.

Then he slid his free arm around Poppy and

scooped her in for a quick kiss, sending her emotions spinning in another direction.

"Well done."

"We haven't seen the bees yet," she pointed out, wobbling between delirious happiness and intense longing. She worried often that his feelings toward her were still very superficial, but if he was willing to give her this—not just the castle above it, but the space to explore the creativity inside her—surely that meant he cared for her on a deeper level?

"By all means, let's go see the bees," Rico said magnanimously, oblivious to her conflict. "If there are birds to go with them, I'm sold."

"Your daddy thinks he's funny," she told Lily, trying to hide her insecurities.

"Da." Lily poked him in the cheek.

"Dada, yes." He caught her hand in his big one and kissed the point of her tiny finger. "You're as smart as your mama, aren't you?" He kissed Poppy again. "Yes?"

She shakily nodded.

Rico called to make an offer before they

left. A week later, Poppy added meetings with interior designers and landscape contractors to her already busy weeks.

Even with those small successes, she was hideously nervous when she finished dressing for the Montero gala. It was an annual event, one that Sorcha and Rico's mother hosted on alternate years. Sorcha had told her what she had spent on her own gown and said, "Match it. This is your debut as a Montero." Then she had sent her favorite designer to the penthouse to consult with Poppy.

Poppy turned in the mirror, feeling like the biggest fraud in the world. Who was that woman? Had she gone too demure? The gown had a high neck and cap sleeves, but the fitted bodice accentuated her curves. The top was a very dramatic gold satin with a floral pattern in carmine and saffron and chestnut. The skirt was an A-line in crimson silk that moved like pouring paint, graceful and luxurious, following her in a small train even after she put on five-inch heels.

Her final touch was an art deco bracelet the

stylist had recommended. Poppy, neophyte that she was, hadn't realized the stones were genuine sapphires and topaz and the gold twenty-four karat until the woman had looked up from her phone with excitement.

"Your husband signed off on it. He *does* want to make a statement, doesn't he?"

Poppy had smiled wanly, head swimming at what she'd accidentally bought.

She felt light-headed now as she walked out to the lounge, wondering what he would make of all of this, especially her hair. It had been straightened to within an inch of its life, then a slip of gold ribbon woven through a waterfall braid around her crown.

Rico paused with his drink halfway to his mouth.

She wrinkled her nose and took a slow turn, corkscrewing the skirt around her. *Super sophisticated, Poppy. Don't try that again.* She gave it a small ruffle to straighten it then stood tall, facing him again.

He hadn't moved.

"What's wrong?" She started searching for the flaw.

"Absolutely nothing." He set aside his drink and came to her, lifted the hand with the bracelet. "You look stunning."

"Really? Thank you. You look really nice, too." A tuxedo, for heaven's sake. She covered her racing heart. "Are we solving an international crime this evening?"

Someone was definitely targeting his heart. Rico almost said it, but it was too close to the truth.

She looked up at him and he read the sensual awareness that was always there between them, ready to be stoked into flame. There was a glow from deeper within her, too. One that was wide and bright and hot, like the sun about to rise behind the mountains and pierce through him.

It was beautiful, making him catch his breath in a strange anticipation, but he made himself break eye contact and move them out the door.

He was still trying to find the middle ground between providing Poppy the supportive attention she craved and maintaining some sort of governance over himself. He recalled chiding his brother once for having affection for Sorcha. *You don't want to admit you have a weakness where she's concerned.*

It was a weakness. Not only of character. It was a vulnerability that could be exploited so he steeled himself against allowing his affections to run too deep.

Even so, he found himself eager to show her off. He'd never been one of those men who wore a woman like a badge of virility, but apparently, he was capable of being that guy.

The pride swelling his chest and straining the buttons of his pleated shirt wasn't really about how Poppy made *him* look, though. Hell yes, he stood taller when he escorted her into the marquise behind Cesar's villa. But he stuck close to her not to be seen with her, or even to protect her—which he would in a heartbeat if anyone stepped out of line.

No, he was enjoying watching the way her

confidence was blossoming. He couldn't change his world to make it easier for her to fit into it, but seeing her grow more comfortable with these trappings pleased him. *Eased* him.

She smiled and greeted couples she had already met and calmly ignored the occasional sideways glance from people still digesting the gossip that Rico Montero had married the mother of his love child.

She even showed less anxiety when they caught up with his parents, exchanging air kisses with his mother and speaking with genuine enthusiasm about the new house. She had clearly been studying at Sorcha's knee because she then asked his mother, "Would you have time next week to review the floor plan with me? Sorcha assures me I'll need the space for entertaining, but I don't want the front room to feel like a barn."

"Email my assistant. I'm sure she can find an hour for you."

It sounded like a slight, but the fact his mother

was willing to make time for her was a glow-ing compliment.

"You're building a darkroom," Rico's fa-ther said.

"Yes." Poppy faltered briefly with surprise, then tried her newfound strategy on him. "I wondered if you could advise me on where best to source the chemicals?"

"Your husband can do that."

Rico bit back a sigh. He held Poppy's elbow cradled in his palm and lightly caressed her inner arm while saying, "It's not always clear whether my father is genuinely interested or merely being polite." *Be polite*, he transmit-ted with a hard look into his father's profile.

"Rico," his mother murmured, her own stern expression reminding him they were all aware of his father's limitations. And they were in *public*.

"I am interested." Rico's father frowned, being misinterpreted. "Keep me apprised of your progress," he ordered Poppy. "I'd like to observe the process when you're up to full function. La Reina, I've seen people we ought to speak to."

"Of course." They melted into the crowd.

"Wow," Poppy said as they moved away. She slapped a bright smile on her face, but he saw through to the woman who felt ground into the dust.

"This is why the house you found us is so perfect." He stroked her bare arms. "It's even farther away from them than this one."

Her hurt faded and her mouth twitched. "That's not nice."

"No. And you don't realize it, but he was being as nice as he gets. His asking to observe you is quite the commendation."

"Really?" She dipped her chin, skeptical.

"Mmm-hmm. If I cared about scoring points with my parents, I would be high-fiving you right now."

"We could dance instead," Poppy suggested. "What's wrong?"

"Nothing." Except he'd just recalled the steps he was taking that, as far as scoring points with his parents went, would wipe him to below zero in their books. He would owe future favors. *That* was the cost of giving in to base feelings like passion and infatuation.

So he wouldn't.

"Let's dance," he murmured and drew her onto the floor.

CHAPTER NINE

POPPY WAS FALLING for Rico. Really falling. This wasn't the secret crush of a maid for a man who hadn't even noticed her. It wasn't the sexual infatuation of a woman whose husband left her weak with satisfaction every night. It wasn't even the tender affinity of shared love for their daughter, although what she was feeling had its roots in all of those things.

This was the kind of regard her grandparents had felt for each other. She knew because she began doing the sorts of little things for Rico that they used to do for one another. If he tried a particular brandy while they were out, and liked it, she asked the housekeeper to order some in. When discussing the decor of his home office in the new house, she had the designer track down a signed print of his favorite racecar driver, now retired but still revered.

And when she had an appointment to spend the morning looking at photography equipment, she impulsively called Rico's assistant and asked if her husband had plans for lunch. He was pronounced available so she booked herself as his date and made a reservation, dropping in to surprise him.

His PA, a handsome man about her age whom she was meeting in person for the first time, rose to greet her. He looked startled. Alarmed. Maybe even appalled.

"Senora Montero. You're early." He smoothed his expression to a warm and welcoming smile. "I'm Anton. So good to meet you. Why don't I show you around while Senor Montero finishes his meeting?"

Poppy might be a country girl at heart, but she knew a slick city hustle when she was the victim of one. She balked, heart going into free fall. All her optimistic belief that she and Rico were making progress in their marriage disintegrated. One dread-filled question escaped her.

"Who is he with?"

Before Anton could spit out a suitable prevarication, the door to Rico's office cracked. He came out with an older couple. Everyone wore somber expressions.

Rico's face tightened with regret when he saw her. Anton offered a pinched smile of apology. He moved quickly to the closet where the older woman's light coat had been hung.

The older couple both stiffened, clearly recognizing her while Poppy's brain scrambled and somehow made the connection that they must be Faustina's parents.

The brief anguish she had suffered mildewed into horror. Rico wasn't meeting some Other Woman. *She* was that reviled creature.

How did one act in such a profoundly uncomfortable moment? What should she say? All she could conjure was the truth.

"I wanted to surprise you," she admitted to Rico, voice thick with apology. "I didn't realize you would be tied up." She thought she might be sick.

Rico introduced her to the Cabreras. Neither put out their hand to shake so Poppy kept her own clutched over her purse, nodding and managing a small smile that wasn't returned.

"The woman you 'dated very briefly when your engagement was interrupted,'" Faustina's mother said with a dead look in her eye.

"I'm very sorry," Poppy choked, reminding herself that they had lost their only child and would hurt forever because of it.

"I'm sure you are," Senora Cabrera said bitterly. "Despite gaining all the prestige and wealth my daughter brought to this marriage. What do *you* bring except cheap notoriety and a bastard conceived in adultery?"

Poppy gasped and stumbled slightly as Rico scooped her close, pressing her to stand more behind him than beside him.

"The hypocrisy is mine. Don't take your anger out on Poppy." His tone was so dark and dangerous, she curled a fist into the fabric of his jacket in a useless effort to restrain him, fearing he would physically attack them. "Leave innocent babies out of this altogether."

A profound silence, then Senora Cabrera sniffed with affront. Her husband clenched his teeth so hard, Poppy could have sworn she heard them crunching like hard candy behind the flat line of his lips.

"I've given you some options," Rico continued in a marginally more civilized voice. "Let me know how you'd like to proceed."

"Options," Senor Cabrera spat. "None that are worth accepting. This is hell," he told Rico forcefully. "You have sent us to hell, Rico. I hope you're happy."

The older man whirled and jerked his head at his wife. She hurried after him. Anton trotted to catch up and escort them to the elevator while Rico swore quietly and viciously as he strode back into his office.

Poppy followed on apprehensive feet, quietly closing the door and pressing her back against it. She watched him pour a drink.

"I am *so* sorry. Anton didn't tell me they would be here or I wouldn't have come. I asked him not to tell you I was dropping in. This is all my fault."

"I knew you were coming." He threw back a full shot. "I thought we would be finished an hour ago. It went long—you were early. Bad timing." He poured a second. "Do you want one?"

"It was that bad?" She wondered how many he'd had before talking to the older couple. Maybe she ought to make some espresso with that machine behind the bar.

"It was difficult." He poured two glasses and brought them to the low table where melting ice water and full cups of coffee sat next to untouched plates of biscotti. He set the fresh glasses into the mix and threw himself into an armchair.

She lowered herself to the sofa, briefly taking in the classic decor of the office with its bookshelves and antique desk. A younger version of Senor Cabrera looked down in judgment from a frame on the wall. She felt utterly helpless. Deserving of blame, yet Rico wasn't casting any, just slouching there, brooding.

"What sort of options did you give them?" She hated to ask, sensing by their animosity his suggestions hadn't been well received.

"I told them I was stepping down."

"From being president?" A jolt went through her. It was the last thing she had expected. "Why?"

"I have to." He frowned as if it was obvious. "I had my parents prepare them for it when they informed them about you and Lily. I've stayed to keep things on an even keel, but today I gave them the alternatives for transitioning me out of the chair."

She could only blink, remembering what he had told her in the solarium the day Faustina had broken his engagement. Poppy hadn't meant to pry, but she had admitted to not understanding the appeal of an arranged marriage. She had been compelled to ask what he would have gained.

I was to become president of Faustina's father's chemical research firm. Cesar and I work very well together, but this would have given me a playground for my personal proj-

ects and ambitions. My chance to shine in my own spotlight.

He'd been self-deprecating, but she had sensed a real desire in him to prove something, if only to himself. She completely understood that. It was akin to what drove her interest in photography.

"What will you do?" she asked now.

"Go back to working under Cesar. There's always room for me there."

But it wasn't what he wanted. "You married Faustina so you could move out from his shadow. You have your own ambitions."

"I'll find another way to pursue them." He flicked his hand, dismissing that desire.

"But—" She frowned. "What happens with this company? Do they become your competitors again?"

"One option is to leave this enterprise under Cesar's direction. Another would be for us to sell this back to them at a discounted price. They'd be gaining a much more lucrative business than when I took over." He muttered into his glass. "So I think that's what they'll choose."

"How much would it impact you if they do? Financially, I mean?" Her blood was congealing in her veins. They'd just bought a house. Not a cute bungalow in a small prairie town that a union wage could pay off in twenty years, but a mansion with acres of grapes and the sort of view that cost more than the house. Her palms were sweating. "Why didn't you tell me this was happening?"

"Because it doesn't affect you. The sting in the pocketbook will be short-lived, some legal fees and a return of some stocks and other holdings. I'll have to restructure my personal portfolio, but our family has weathered worse. Things will balance out."

She could only sit there with a knot of culpability in her middle.

"Rico, I hate that I brought nothing to this marriage. I didn't know I was going to *cost* you. Not like this." Her eyes grew hot and she braced her elbows on her knees to cover her eyes with her palms. "I've been spending like a drunken sailor. I just ordered equipment for— I'll call them. Cancel it." She looked for her purse.

"Poppy." He leaned forward and caught her wrist. "Don't take this the wrong way, but a few thousand euros on photography equipment isn't going to make a dent in what's about to change hands. Cesar and I have discussed how to finance this. You and I are perfectly fine."

"But this is my fault! Now he's going to hate me, too. Sorcha will stop being my friend. I'm sorry, Rico. I'm so sorry I slept with you and ruined everything."

Her words hit his ears in a crash, like the avalanche of rocks off a cliff that continued roaring and tumbling long after the first crack of thunder, leaving a whiff of acrid dust in the air.

They came on top of words spoken by Señora Cabrera that had made him see red. *A bastard conceived in adultery.*

That was not what Lily was. Their attack

against Poppy had been equally blood boiling and now *Poppy* was expressing regret over their daughter's conception?

"Don't you *dare* say that."

Maybe it was the alcohol hitting his system, maybe it was the pent-up tension from his meeting releasing in a snap. Maybe it was simply that he was confronted with Poppy's emotions so often, he was beginning to tap into his own, but rather than suppress his anger, he let himself feel it. It raged through him because her words *hurt*.

"I told you I will never regard Lily as a mistake and don't you ever do it, either." He threw himself to his feet, trying to pace away from the burn of scorn that chased him. "I would give up every last penny I possess so long as I can have her in my life."

Damn, that admission made him uncomfortable. He shot her a look and saw her sit back, hand over her chest, tears in her eyes. She was biting her lips together, chin crinkling.

Was he scaring her? He swore and pushed

a hand into his hair, clenching hard enough to feel the pain of it, trying to grapple himself back under control.

"Thank you, Rico," she said in a voice that scraped. "I hope you know that's all I've ever wanted for her. Parents who love her. Not all of this." She flicked a hand around the room.

"I do know that." He swallowed a lump from his throat, but it remained lodged sideways in his chest. He felt pried open and stood there fighting the sensation.

"But I'm starting to see that you and your family support a lot more people than just me and Lily. It shouldn't be such a revelation to me. When I needed a job, your mother gave me one and I was grateful. Now I can see that this lifestyle you're protecting has value to more people than just you. That's why it's upsetting to me that I'm undermining it. I think I'd feel better about it if you'd at least yell at me."

"I'm not going to yell at you." Was he angry? Yes. About many things, but none that mattered as much as his daughter. "My career ambitions and the bearing our marriage has had on them are insignificant next to what I've gained through this marriage. *You brought our child.* There's nothing else you could have brought that comes close to how important she is to me."

There was a flash of something like yearning in her eyes before she screened them with her lashes. She reached to pluck a tissue from the box and pressed it under each eye.

"It means a lot that you would say that. I struggle with exactly what they said. Every day." Her mouth pulled down at the corners. "Feeling like I snuck in through a side door, using my daughter as a ticket. I feel like such an imposter." She sniffed.

"Stop feeling that way," he ordered, coming over to sit beside her, facing her. "It's a terrible thing to say, but I can't imagine Faustina showing our baby the same sort of love that you show Lily. I'm lucky my child has you as her mother."

Her eyes grew even bigger and swam with even more tears. Her mouth trembled in earnest.

"Please don't cry. You're making me feel like a jerk."

"You're being the opposite of a jerk. That's why I'm crying."

She had worn her hair in a low ponytail today and half of it was coming loose around her face. He wound a tendril around his finger, thinking of how often he saw her wince and pry Lily's fist from the mass, never scolding her for it.

How could anyone resist this mass, though? He dipped his head to rub the ribbon of silk against his lips. Watched her gaze drop to his mouth and tried not to get distracted.

"There's something I've been wanting to ask you," Rico began.

Her gaze flashed upward, brimming with inquisitive light. "Yes?"

Unnatural, fearful hope filled him even as he second-guessed what was on his tongue. He couldn't believe these words were forming inside him. Not as the next strategic move in the building of the Montero empire, either. Not in reaction to what outsiders said about their marriage. No, this was something that had been bubbling in him from the earliest days of their marriage, something he didn't want to examine too closely because it occupied such a deep cavern inside him.

"Rico?" she prompted.

"With the house almost ready, I keep thinking we should talk about filling more of those rooms."

Her pupils threatened to swallow her face. "Another baby?"

"I know you wanted to wait." He let go of her hair and covered the hand that went limp against his thigh. He pressed his lips together, bracing himself for rebuff. "If you're not ready, we can table it, but I wanted to mention it. My relationship with Pia and Cesar— we're not as close as some, but I value them. I realize many things contribute to the distance between you and your half-siblings, but the age gap is a factor. That's why I thought sooner than later would benefit Lily."

He heard his upbringing in the logic of his argument and recognized it as the defense tactic it was. If he kept his feelings firmly out of the discussion, there was no chance they would get trampled on.

Poppy blinked and a fresh tear hit her cheek, diamond bright. "Are you being serious? You want to make a baby with me *on purpose*?"

The magnitude wasn't lost on him. Marriages could be undone. Property could be split. The entanglement of a child—*children*, if he had any say in it—was a far bigger and more permanent commitment.

"I do."

"You didn't tell me there's such a thing as a babymoon," Rico said a month later as they toured the empty rooms of their villa, inspecting freshly painted walls, window treatments and light fixtures. Furniture delivery would start next week.

"You'd have seen one by now if you had

ever changed a diaper," she teased. "Instead of handing Lily off to the nanny."

Rico's mouth twitched, but he only drew her onto the private balcony off their master bedroom. It made her feel like the queen of the world to stand there looking so far out on the Mediterranean she was sure she glimpsed the cowboy boot of Italy.

"Besides, we're not there yet."

After a visit to the doctor a couple of weeks ago, they were officially "trying." Today, Rico had asked the designer about setting up a nursery *when the time comes.* The woman had cheerfully promised a quick turnaround on redecorating the room of their choice. "Most couples take a babymoon for a few weeks so we aren't disrupting their daily life," the woman had added, then had to explain to Rico what it was.

"We never even had a honeymoon," he pointed out now.

"There's been a lot going on. A lot for Lily to adjust to. I wouldn't want to leave her even now, when we're about to move into this house and change everything again."

"We could take her with us."

"I think that's called a family vacation, not a honeymoon."

"You're full of cheek today, aren't you?" He gave one of her lower ones a friendly squeeze. "We could take the nanny so we get our alone time. Really put our back into the honeymoon effort. See if we can't earn ourselves a baby-moon."

She chuckled. "So romantic." But she kissed him under his chin, ridiculously in love when he was playful like this—

Oh. There it was. The acknowledgment she'd been avoiding. Because if she admitted to herself that she was fully head over heels, she had to face that he wasn't.

"Romance is not my strong point, but sound logic is."

He gathered her so her arms were folded against his chest, fingertips grazing his open collar, but his words echoed through the hollow spaces growing wider in her chest.

"The transition is almost finished with the Cabreras," he continued. "Cesar has some projects he wants me to take the lead on in a couple of months. I won't have much down-time once I'm knee-deep. This is our window for a getaway. Let's take it."

"If you want to," she murmured, thinking she ought to feel happy. Excited. But she only felt sad. She felt the way she had as a child, wishing her mother and father wanted her. It shouldn't have mattered. She'd been loved by her grandparents.

But she'd still felt the absence of it from people she thought *should* love her.

And she felt it again now.

"What's wrong?"

"Nothing," she lied, conjuring a smile. "Where…? Um…where would you want to go?"

"I don't know. Somewhere that Lily would enjoy and you could play with your new camera. Maybe we could tie in a visit to your grandmother at the end. I know you're missing her."

"You wouldn't mind?"

"Of course not. I wish she would agree to come live with us here. You know you can visit her anytime. I'll come with you as often as I can."

"Thank you." A tiny spark of hope returned. Whenever he doted on her, she thought maybe he *was* coming to love her. Tentative light crept through her. "Okay. Let's do it."

Two weeks later, they were riding elephants through the rainforests of Thailand.

"This is not camping," she told him when they arrived at the hidden grotto where sleep pods were suspended in the trees. "Camping is digging a trench around your tent in a downpour at midnight so you don't drown in your sleep."

"I think this is 'glamping,'" the nanny murmured in an aside as the pod she would share with Lily was pointed out to her. "And *thank you*."

They dined on rare mushrooms and wild boar, coconut curry soup and tropical fruit with cashews. When they fell asleep, replete from lovemaking, the wind rocked their pod and the frogs crooned a lullaby. They woke to strange birdcalls and the excited trumpet of a baby elephant as it trampled into a mud pool.

Poppy caught some of the elephant's antics with her new toy, a Leica M6. She switched out to her new digital camera to catch some shots of Lily to send to Gran then held her as she fed the baby elephant, chuckling as Lily squealed in delight.

A click made her look up and she found Rico capturing them on his phone.

"New screen saver," he said as he tucked it away.

Poppy flushed with pleasure, in absolute heaven. She began to think she really was living happily-ever-after, cherished by her husband, making a family with him. Her life couldn't be more ideal.

Then, as they came off their last day in the forest to stay a few days at a luxury beach resort on the coast, she discovered that, for all their success the first time, they weren't so lucky this time. She wasn't one-and-done pregnant.

It wasn't even the light spotting that had fooled her with Lily. She had a backache and a heavier than normal case of the blues.

Plenty of women didn't conceive right away. There was no reason she should take it this hard. She knew that in her head, but her heart was lying there in two jagged pieces anyway.

Rico came into the bedroom of their suite as she was coming out of the bathroom.

"I sent the nanny to the beach with Lily. We—" He took off his sunglasses and frowned. "What's wrong?"

He wore a T-shirt and shorts better than any man she'd ever met. The shirt clung to his sculpted shoulders and chest and his legs were tanned and muscled. One of her favorite things in the world was the scrape of his fine hair when she ran the inside of her thigh against his iron-hard ones.

Everything about him was perfect.

And she wasn't. She hadn't even gotten this right.

"It's not working. I'm not pregnant."

"Oh." He was visibly taken aback. "You're sure?"

She bit back a tense, *Of course I'm sure*, and only said, "Yes." She turned her back and threw sunscreen and a few other things into a beach bag.

"But it only took once last time."

"I know that." She drew a patience-gathering breath. "I don't know why it didn't happen." She blinked, fighting tears. "But it didn't and there's nothing I can do about it."

"Poppy." He touched her arm. "It's fine. We're having fun trying, right? Next time."

She didn't want him to be disappointed. That would make her feel worse. But it didn't help to hear him brush it off, either. She dug through her bag, unable to remember if she'd thrown her book in there.

"You go. I'll catch up."

"Poppy. Come on. Don't be upset. This isn't a test that we have to pass or fail."

"Not for you it isn't. For me? Yes it is. Every

single day! Either I bring value to this marriage or I'm just a hanger-on."

"I have *never* meant to make you feel like that."

"I feel like that because that's what I *am*." The rope handle of her bag began to cut into her shoulder. She threw the whole works onto the floor, standing outside herself and knowing this was toddler-level behavior, but there was poison sitting deep inside her. The kind that had to come out before it turned her completely septic. "At least when I was looking after my grandparents, I was *contributing*. You don't need me to look after Lily. The nanny does most of the work."

"You *love* Lily. I told you that's all—"

"Yes! I love her. That's what I bring. The ability to give you babies and love them. Except now there's no baby." She flung out a hand.

"We've just started trying! Look." He attempted to take her by the shoulders, but she brushed him off and backed away. "Poppy. I don't know much about this process, but I do know it takes some couples a while. There is no need to be this upset."

"I *want* to be upset!" She hated how backed into a corner she felt. She pushed past him and strode to the middle of the room only to spin around and confront. "But I'm not allowed to be upset, am I? There's no such thing as emotion in your world, is there? I'm supposed to fit into a tiny little box labeled Wife and Mother." She made a square with her hands. "And uphold the family image, except I'll never be able to do that because I'm forever going to be a blotch."

"Calm down," he ordered.

She flung out a hand in a silent, *There it is.*

He heard it, too, and sighed. He gave her a stern look. "You're not a blotch. We've been over all of this. You contribute. I don't know why you struggle to believe that."

"Because I've been a burden my entire life, Rico. My grandparents were planning to do things in their retirement. Take bus tours and travel and *see* things. Instead, they were stuck raising me."

"It didn't sound to me like that was how your grandmother felt."

"That's still how it *was*. That's how I wound up working in your mother's house. I couldn't bear the thought of asking them for money when they'd supported me all those years. Then I came home and bam. Pregnant. Back to being a parasite. Gramps didn't want to sell that house because he was afraid I would go broke paying day care and rent. I was supposed to pay Gran back after all those years she took care of me, but now you're supporting her. *And* me. That feels *great*."

"You are not a parasite. Eleanor is my daughter's great-grandmother. I *want* to look after her. And you."

"See, that's it." She lifted a helpless hand. "Right there. You don't want to look after *me*." She pressed her hand to the fissure in her chest where all her emotions were bleeding out and making a mess on the floor. "You want to look after Lily's mother. Exactly the way they took in their son's daughter for his sake. You don't want *me*, Rico."

"You're upset. Taking things to heart that don't require this much angst."

Her heart was the problem. That much he had right. It felt like her heart was beating outside her chest.

"Do you love me?" she asked, already knowing the answer. "Do you think you're ever going to love me?"

Her question gave him pause. The fact a watchful expression came across his face as he searched for a response that was kind yet truthful was all the answer she needed.

"Because I love you," she admitted, feeling no sense of relief as the words left barbs in her throat. Her lips were so wobbly, her speech was almost slurred. "I love you so much I ache inside, all the time. I want so badly to be enough for you—"

"You are," he cut in gruffly.

"Well, you're not enough for me!" The statement burst out of her, breaking something open in her. Between them. All the delicate filaments that had connected them turned to dust, leaving him pallid. Leaving her throat arid and the rest of her blistered with self-hatred as she threw herself on the pyre, adding, "This isn't enough."

His breath hissed in.

"At least my grandparents loved me, despite the fact I'd been dumped on them. But I waited my whole childhood for my parents to want me. To love me. I can't live like that again, Rico. I can't take up space in your home because your children need a mother. I need more. And what breaks my heart is knowing that you're capable of it. You love Lily. I know you do. But you don't love me and you won't and *that's not fair.*"

He let her go.

He shouldn't have let her walk out, but he didn't know what to say. He knew what she wanted to hear him say, but those words had never passed his lips.

From his earliest recollection of hearing the phrase, when he realized other children said those words to their parents, he had instinctively understood it wasn't a sentiment his own parents would want to hear from him. They weren't a family who said such a thing. They weren't supposed to feel it. Or *want* to feel it.

So he let her walk out and close the door with a polite click that sounded like the slam of a vault, locking him out of something precious he had only glimpsed for a second.

Which seemed to empty him of his very soul.

He looked around, recalling dimly that he'd thought to enjoy an afternoon delight before joining their daughter on the beach for sand castles and splashing in the waves.

Not pregnant. He had to admit that had struck harder than he would have expected. It left a hole in his chest that he couldn't identify well enough to plug. He knew how to manage his expectations. He'd spent his entire life keeping his low, so as not to suffer disappointment or loss. Despite that, he was capable of both. He wanted to go after Poppy and ask again, *Are you sure?*

She was sure. The bleak look in her eyes

had kicked him in the gut. He wasn't ready to face that again. That despair had nearly had him telling her they didn't have to try again ever, not if a lack of conception was going to hit her so hard it broke something in her.

He wanted a baby, though. The compulsion to build on what they had was beyond voracious. How could Poppy not realize she was an integral part of this new sense of family he was only beginning to understand?

Family wasn't what he'd been taught— loyalty and rising to responsibility, sharing a common history and acting for the good of the whole. That was part of it, but family was also a smiling kiss greeting him when he walked in the door. It was a trusting head on his shoulder and decisions made together. It was a sense that he could relax. That he would be judged less harshly by those closest to him. His mistakes would be forgiven.

Forgive me, he thought despairingly.

And heard her say again, *You're not enough for me.*

He was still trying to find his breath after

that one. He knew how it felt to be accepted on condition, better than she realized. The gold standard for approval in his childhood had been a mastery over his emotions. Tears were weakness, passion vulgar. He should only go after things that made sense, that benefited the family, not what he *wanted*.

Do you love me?

He didn't know how. That was the bitter truth.

He would give Poppy nearly anything she asked for, but he refused to say words to her that weren't sincere. How the hell would he know one way or the other if what he felt was love, though? He hadn't had any exposure to that elusive emotion, not until his brother had gone off the rails with Sorcha, causing his parents to shrink in horror, further reinforcing to Rico that deep emotions prompted destructive madness.

Love had *killed* Faustina, for God's sake.

He hated himself for hurting Poppy, though. For failing her. The sick ache sat inside him as he went out and looked for her. She wasn't on a lounger under the cabana with the nanny, watching Lily play in a shaded pocket of sand.

He moved to stand near them, scanning for Poppy, figuring she would turn up here eventually.

It took him a moment to locate her, walking in the wet sand where waves washed ashore and retreated. Was she crying? She looked so desolate on that empty stretch so far from the cheerful crowd of the resort beach.

She wasn't a burden. It killed him that her parents had let her grow up feeling anything less than precious. She brought light into darkness, laughter into sober rooms.

She had brought him Lily—literally life. He glanced at his daughter. She was batting down each of the castles the nanny made for her. The most enormous well-being filled him whenever he was anywhere near this little sprite. Poppy shone like the sun when she was with Lily, clearly the happiest she could possibly be.

That was why he wanted another baby. He didn't know how to express what he felt for

Poppy except to physically make another of these joy factories. With her. He wanted her to have more love. The best of himself, packaged new and flawless, without the jagged edges and rusted wheels. Clean, perfect, unconditional love.

From him.

He swallowed, hands in fists as he absorbed that he may not know how to love, how to express it, but it was inside him. He would die for Lily and if Poppy was hurting, he was hurting.

He couldn't bear that. Not for one more minute.

He looked for her again, intent on going after her.

She had wandered even farther down the beach, past the flags and signage that warned of—

He began jogging after her, to call her back.

Long before he got there, the sea reached with frothy arms that gathered around her legs and dragged her in. One second she was there, the next she was gone.

"Poppy!" he hollered at the top of his lungs and sprinted down the beach.

One moment she was wading along, waves breaking on her shins. Without warning, the water swirled higher. It dragged with incredible strength against her thighs, eroding the sand from beneath her feet at the same time. The dual force knocked her off-balance and she fell, splooshing under.

It shocked her out of her morose tears, but she knew how to swim. She mostly felt like an idiot, tumbling like a drunk into the surf. As she sputtered to the surface, she glanced around, hoping no one had witnessed her clumsiness.

As she tried to get her feet under her, however, she couldn't find the bottom. She was in far deeper water than she ought to be. As she gave a little dog paddle to get back toward the beach, she realized she was being sucked away from it. Fast.

Panic struck in a rush of adrenaline. She willed herself not to give in to it. This was a rip current. She only knew one thing about them and that was to swim sideways out of it.

She tried, but the beach was disappearing quickly, making her heart beat even quicker. Her swimsuit wrap was dragging and tangling on her arms. When she tried to call out for help, she caught a mouthful of salt water and was so far away, no one would hear her anyway.

Terrified, she flipped onto her back, floating and kicking, trying to get her bearings while she wrestled herself free of the wrap and caught her breath.

Think, think, think.

Oh, dear God. She popped straight and the people were just the size of ants. Had anyone even noticed she'd been swept out? She looked for a boat. Were there sharks? *Don't panic.*

She was beyond where the waves were breaking. This was where surfers would usually gather, sitting on their boards as they watched the hump of waves, picking and choosing which to ride into shore.

She didn't know how to bodysurf, though. It was all she could do to keep her head up as the waves picked her up and rolled toward the beach without her.

Treading water, she saw nothing, only what looked like a very long swim to shore. She thought she might be on the far side of the current that had carried her out. A crosscurrent was drifting her farther toward the headland, away from where she'd left Lily on the beach.

Lily. She tried not to cry. Lily was safe, she reminded herself.

This was such a stupid mess to be in. She had picked a fight with Rico then walked away to sulk. Why? What did she have to complain about? He treated her like a queen. No one she knew took tropical vacations and rode elephants and slept in five-star ocean-front villas with butler service to the beach.

I'm sorry, baby, she said silently as she began to crawl her arms over her head, aiming for the headland that was a lot farther than she'd ever swum in her life. A few laps in a pool were her limit. Just enough to get her safety badge when she was ten. *I'm sorry, Rico. Please, Gramps, if you can hear me, I need help.*

Rico absconded with a Jet Ski, scaring an adolescent boy into giving it up with whatever expression was on his face. The only words he'd had in him had been a grated, "My wife."

Her coral wrap had been his beacon as he raced to the family with the Jet Skis. Now it was gone.

He ran the Jet Ski along the edge of the riptide, gaze trying to penetrate the cloudy water, searching for a glint of color, of red hair, terrified he'd find her in it and terrified he wouldn't.

He sped out to where the head of the current mushroomed beyond the surf zone, dissipating in a final cloud of sand pulled from the beach. Still nothing.

Dimly he noted two surfers and a lifeguard from the resort joining his search, zigzagging through the surf.

He had to find her. *Had to.*

In a burst of speed, he started down the far side of the rip and had to fight the Jet Ski to get back toward the current. Another one, not as strong, ran parallel to the beach. He realized she might have been drawn toward the headland. It was a huge stretch of water to get there.

Despair began to sink its claws into him.

Bill, help us out, he silently begged her grandfather's spirit.

A glint above the water caught his attention. A drone?

He looked toward the beach and saw the operator waving him toward the headland.

Using the drone as a beacon, he gunned the Jet Ski that direction, searched the chop of waves. *Please, please, please.*

A slender arm slowly came out of the water. It windmilled in a tired backstroke, slapping wearily on reentry.

Swearing, he raced toward her. The resignation in her eyes as she spotted him told him how close she'd been to giving up. He got near enough she put a hand on the machine, but he had to turn it off and get in the water with her to get her onto it, she was that weak.

She sat in front of him, trembling and coughing, breaths panting and heart hammering through her back into his own slamming in his chest. She hunched weakly while he reached to start the Jet Ski again. He shifted her slightly so he could hold on to her and steered it back to shore.

He was shaking. Barely processing anything other than that he had to get them to dry land.

"I'm sorry," she said when he got to the small dock where the startled family had gathered with damned near every living soul in Thailand.

The crowd gave them a round of applause. The nanny stood with Lily on her hip, eyes wide with horror at the barely averted catastrophe.

"Oh, Lily," Poppy sobbed, and hugged her daughter, but Lily squirmed at her mother's wet embrace.

A lifeguard came to check on Poppy.

"Have a hot shower. You'll be in shock. Lie down and stay warm. Drink lots of water to flush the seawater you drank."

Rico nodded and took her into their villa, bringing her straight into the shower and starting it, peeling off their wet clothes as they stood under the spray.

"I'm so sorry," she said, feeling like she was drowning all over again as the fresh water poured like rain upon them.

He dragged at the tie on her bikini top only to tighten the knot. He turned her and she felt his fingers between her shoulder blades, picking impatiently at the knot.

"I wasn't paying attention. It was stupid. I'm really sorry. Please don't think I did that on purpose. I was upset, but I wouldn't leave Lily. I know she needs me."

"I need you!" he shouted, making her jump.

She turned around and backed into the tiles, catching the loosened top so she clutched the soggy, hanging cups against her cold breasts.

"You scared the hell out of me. I thought—" His face spasmed and she saw drops on his cheeks that might have been from the shower, but might have been something else. "What would I do without you, Poppy?"

He cupped her face and the incendiary light in his eyes was both fury and something else. Something that made her hold her breath as he tenderly pressed his thumbs to the corners of her mouth.

"I wanted to go looking for you the day after the solarium. Do you know that? I didn't know where to start. Ask the staff? It was too revealing. Try to catch you at the hostel? The airport? You hadn't told me the name of the town where you lived, but I imagined I could find out. I didn't want to wait that long or travel that far, though. Not if I could catch you before you left."

He was talking in a voice so thick and heavy with anguish it made her ache.

"It was an irrational impulse, Poppy. We don't have those in this family. I couldn't admit to *myself* how attracted I was. I couldn't let anyone else see it, not even you. I had to live up to my responsibilities. After Cesar, *I* had to show some sense. It was better to let you go. *But I didn't want to.*"

Her mouth trembled. "Then Faustina took away any choice you might have."

"Yes." He moved his hands to lift the bathing suit cups off her chest and high enough to pull the tie free from behind her neck.

Her hair fell in wet tendrils onto her shoulders. He drew her back under the spray, took a squirt of fragrant body wash in his palm and turned her to rub the warm lather over her back and shoulders, working heat into her tired, still trembling muscles.

"Everything in my world went gray. Through the wedding, into my marriage and after she was gone. I didn't care about anything. I had achieved maximum indifference." His hands dug their soapy massage into her muscles, strong and reassuring. "Then Sorcha told me you might have had my baby. I tried to approach the situation rationally. I did. But the test came back inconclusive and I got on the plane. I had to see you. I had to know."

"What if Lily hadn't been yours?"

He turned her. A faint smile touched his mouth. "Can you imagine? There I was spitting fire and fury and you might have said she was Ernesto's."

"The seventy-year-old gardener? Yes, he's always been my type."

He turned her to settle her back against his chest. He ran his firm palms across her upper chest and down her arms, not trying to arouse, but the warmth tingling through her held flickers of the desire that always kindled when they were close.

"I have a feeling it wouldn't have mattered if she wasn't mine." His voice was a grave rumble in his chest. A somber vow against her ear. "I can't see myself turning around and going home just because I happened to be wrong. One way or another, you were meant to be here in my life. I was meant to be Lily's father."

She swallowed, astonished. Shaken. Questioning whether this man of logic really believed in fate.

"You're talking like your bohemian wife who thinks her grandfather can talk to her through the stars."

His hand slowed and his chin rested against her hair. "You think I didn't ask him for help? Did you see the drone above you?"

"No. But that would be a tourist, not Gramps."

"It was in the sky, Poppy. I was begging him for some sign of you."

He turned her to face him.

Her arms twined themselves around his neck because they knew that was where they belonged. Lather lingered to provide a sensual friction between their torsos.

"I love you." He stared deeply into her eyes as he spoke, allowing her to see all the way to the depths of his soul. To the truth of his statement. "I'm sorry it took something like this for me to say it. To *feel* it. In my defense, it was there—I just didn't know what it was."

She tried to hold it together, but her emotions were still all over the place. Her mouth trembled and tears leaked to join the water hitting her cheeks. "I love you, too." Her voice quavered. "I shouldn't have said you weren't enough. I was upset."

"I know." His gaze grew pained. "Maybe instead of 'trying,' we'll just see. Hmm? I don't want you to think our marriage hinges on whether we have another baby. I love *you*."

"Okay. But I really do want your baby." The yearning and disappointment was still there, but as she let her head rest on his shoulder, the hollowness eased. The darkness was dispelled by the light of his love.

"Me, too." He pressed his wet lips to her crown. "And when the time is right, I'm sure we'll have one."

Weeks later, Rico crowded her to scan the strips of negatives with her.

"I want the one I took of you in front of the waterfall," he said.

Poppy never minded the touch of his body against hers, but, "You're here to tell me how your father will behave. Act like him and pick something he might like."

His parents were coming for an early dinner, their first visit to the finished house. Sorcha and Cesar had plans elsewhere so it would be only the four of them. They would show them the beehives and the wine cellar and, at the explicit request of the duque, Poppy would demonstrate her darkroom.

"The waterfall is a good shot," Rico said, not backing off one hairbreadth. "The ripples in your hair mirrored the path of the water. I've wanted to see it since I took it."

It was poorly framed and crooked, but she could fix that.

Actually, it was a decent shot, she decided, once the negative was in the enlarger. It was perfectly focused and the light was quite pretty, dappling through the jungle leaves. It was taken from behind her. She sat up to her waist in the water, looking toward the waterfall. She had been wearing her bikini and the strings were hidden by the fall of her hair so she looked like a naked nymph spied in her natural habitat.

"I am not showing this one to your father."

She had already run test strips from this batch so she set her timer and switched the overhead light to red. Then she set the paper for exposure.

"How long do we have?" His hands settled on her waist.

"Not long enough." The timer went off and she chuckled at the noise of disappointment that escaped him.

She moved the paper into the developer bath and gently rocked until the second timer pinged. She moved the paper to the fixing bath, explaining as she went.

"This last one is water, to wash off the chemicals." She left the image in the final bath.

"See? It's great," he said.

"It is," she agreed, washing her hands and drying them. "*Now* ask me how much time we have."

"Enough?"

"It shouldn't stay in there more than thirty minutes." She closed one eye and wrinkled her nose. "But we shouldn't stay in *here* more than thirty minutes or we won't have time to get ready for our guests."

"I can work with that."

"I know you can," she purred throatily and held up her arms.

He ambled close, crowded her against the counter beside the sink then lifted her to sit upon it. "Have I told you lately how much I love you?"

Every day. She cradled his hard jaw in soft hands, grazing her lips against the stubble coming in because he hadn't yet shaved. "Have I told you lately that you make all of my dreams come true?"

Maybe not all. They were still "seeing," not "trying," but their love was tender and new. They were protecting it with gentle words and putting no pressure on it with expectations they couldn't control.

"I want to," he said, hands slowing as he ran them over her back and up to pull the thick elastic from her hair. "I want you to be happy."

"I am. So happy I don't know how to contain it all." She skimmed her fingers down to his shirt buttons, good at this now. She smiled as she spread the white shirt. It glowed pink in the red light. She slid light fingers across the pattern of hair flat against thick muscle and drew a circle around his dark nipples.

"Me, too," he said, skimming the strap of her sundress down her shoulder and setting kisses along the tendon at the base of her neck. "I didn't know happiness like this was possible. That it was as simple as opening my heart, loving and allowing myself to be loved. You humble me, being brave enough to teach me that."

This was supposed to be a playful quickie, but his words and the tenderness in his touch were turning it into something far more profound.

"This is what I wanted the day we made love the first time. I wanted to know the man you didn't show to anyone else. Thank you for trusting yourself to me." She held his head in her hands, gazed on the handsome face that she read so easily these days. She pressed her mouth to his.

He took over, gently ravaging in a way that was hungry and passionate and reverent. She responded the way she always did, helplessly and without reserve. She trusted herself to him, too, and it was worth that risk. Their intimacy went beyond the right to open his belt or slide a hand beneath her skirt. His touch was possessive and greedy, but caring and knowing. Hers wasn't hesitant or daring, but confident and welcomed with a growl of appreciation.

He slowed and gazed into her eyes, not because he sensed she needed it, but because, like her, he sensed the magnitude of the moment wrapping around them. Their love would grow over time, but it was real and fixed and imprinted into their souls now. Irrevocable. Unshakable.

They moved in concert, sliding free of the rest of their clothes, losing her panties to a dark corner, drawing close again and *there*. He filled her in a smooth joining that set hot tears of joy to dampen her lashes.

"I love you," she whispered, clinging her arms and legs around him. "I love when we're like this. This is everything."

"Mi amor," he murmured. "You're my heart. My life. Be mine, always."

They moved in the muted struggle of soul mates trying to break the limits of the physical world and become one. For a time, as they moved with synchronicity, mouths sealed and hands chasing shivers across each other's skin, they were nearly there. The rapture held them in a world where only the other existed, where the culmination was a small death to be eluded before the ecstasy of heaven swallowed them whole. Golden light bathed them as they held that delicious shudder of simultaneous orgasm.

Slowly it faded and they drifted back to the earthly world. Poppy came back to awareness of the hard surface where her backside was balanced, the leather of Rico's belt chafing her inner thigh. One bared breast was pressed to his damp chest, his heart still knocking against the swell. His breathing was as unsteady as hers, his arms folded tightly across her back, securing her in her precarious position. She nuzzled her nose in his neck and licked lightly at the salty taste near his Adam's apple.

Within her, he pulsed a final time. She clenched in response.

"I may have a small fetish for the scent of vinegar and sulfur for the rest of my life," he teased, nuzzling her hair. "That was incredible."

She suspected they might have a small something else after this, but she didn't say it. It was only a feeling. An instinct. A premonition she didn't want to jinx.

It proved true a few weeks later.

"Really?" Rico demanded with cautious joy. "It's absolutely confirmed? Because—"

"I know," she assured him, understanding why he was being so careful about getting attached to the idea. She had been wary to believe it, too, despite missing a cycle and having a home test show positive. "But the doctor said yes. I'm pregnant."

He said something under his breath that might have been a curse or a murmur of thanks to a higher power. When he drew her into his embrace, she discovered he was shaking. She felt his chest swell as he consciously took a slow, regulated breath and let it out.

"You're happy?" she guessed, grinning ear to ear, eyes wet as she twined her arms around his waist.

"I want to tell the whole world."

"Most people don't tell anyone until after twelve weeks."

"Can I tell Lily?"

That cracked her up. "Sure. Go ahead."

After a frown of concentration, Lily grabbed a doll by the hair and offered it to Poppy. "Baby."

"Pretty much how I expect my mother to react," Rico drawled. "But at least you and I know what an important occasion this is. Where should we go on our babymoon?"

"I was thinking exotic Saskatchewan?"

"To see your Gran? Excellent idea. But first, come here." He drew her into his lap and kissed her. "I love you."

"I love you, too."

They kissed again and might have let it get a lot steamier, but Lily stuck an arm into the cuddle and said, "Me."

"Yes, I love you, too. Come on." Rico scooped her onto Poppy's lap and kissed the top of his daughter's head. "I don't know where we'll put the new baby, but we'll find room."

EPILOGUE

One year later...

POPPY WATCHED RICO carefully set their infant son in her grandmother's welcoming arms while Poppy's heart swelled so big, she thought it would burst.

"Sé gentil," Lily cautioned her great-grandmother with wide eyes.

"English, button," Rico reminded her, skimming his hand over the rippling red-gold waves. He called Lily button and angel and he called Poppy flash and treasure and keeper of my heart.

"Be gentle," Lily repeated in the near whisper they'd been coaching her to use when her little brother was sleeping. She was two and a half and talking a blue streak in two different languages, sneaking in a little Valencian and the Swiss nanny's French here and there.

"I will be very gentle, my darling," Gran said with a beaming smile and damp eyes. "Will you stand here beside my chair while your mama takes our picture?"

Rico stepped out of the frame, waited while Poppy snapped, then took the camera so she would have a few of her with her grandmother and the children. She didn't let herself wonder how many more chances she would get for photos like this, only embraced that she still had the opportunity today.

"He's beautiful," Gran said, tracing her aged fingertip across the sleep-clenched fist of Guillermo, named for her husband, William. "And heavy," she added ruefully.

"He is," Poppy agreed, gathering up Memo, as Lily was already calling him. Poppy kissed his warm, plump cheek. "Two kilos more than Brenna—that's Sorcha and Cesar's little girl. She's only a couple of weeks younger."

"Brenna is, is, is—" Lily hurried to interject with important information, but hit a wall with her vocabulary.

"Your cousin, sweetheart."

"My cousin," she informed Gran.

"You're very lucky, aren't you? To have a little brother and cousins, too."

"Mateo is bossy."

"Mateo might express similar opinions about his cousin," Rico said with dry amusement, waving Poppy to sit on one end of Gran's small sofa. He took the other and patted his knee for Lily to come into his lap.

Lily relaxed into his chest, head tilted to blink adoringly at her daddy. "Can I see Mateo?"

"In a few days. We're visiting Gran and then we're going camping. Remember?" Poppy said.

"And buy Mateo a toy," Lily recalled.

"That's right. Before we go home, we'll buy toys for him and Enrique."

"And Brenna?"

"And Brenna," Poppy agreed.

"You were so homesick when you first went

to Spain. Now look how happy you are." Eleanor reached out her hand to Rico. He took it in his own. "Thank you for making her smile like this."

"Thank *you*." He secured Lily on his lap as he leaned across to kiss Gran's pale knuckles. "We still have a room in Spain for you," he told her for the millionth time. "It's very warm there."

"I'm too old for migrating around the world like a sea turtle," she dismissed with a wave of her hand. "I have my sister and my friends here. But you're sweet to keep asking."

They stayed through the dinner hour so Gran could show off her great-grandchildren and handsome grandson-in-law.

"Poppy is becoming famous for her photography," Gran made a point of announcing over dessert. "There was a bidding war at the auction."

"It was for charity," Poppy said, blushing and downplaying it. "Rico's brother was being nice, topping each bid."

"Don't be modest. That's not what happened

at all," Rico chided. "Cesar was incensed that people kept trying to outbid him. My sister-in-law wanted it and he wanted her to have it."

"It was so silly," Poppy said, still blushing. "I could have printed her another."

"They wanted the only one and now they have it," Rico said. The negative had been signed and mounted into the frame. "Poppy has an agent and is filling out her portfolio. We expect she'll have her first show next year. We're heading north in the morning, hoping to catch the aurora borealis."

The whole table said, "Ooh."

The next night, they were ensconced in a resort that billed itself as one of the best places for viewing the northern lights. Their children were abed, the nanny reading a book by the fire and Poppy and Rico were tramping through the trees to a lake that reflected the stars and the sky.

The world was still and monochromatic under the moonlight, the air crisp with the coming fall. They stood holding hands a long moment, absorbing the silence.

"Well, Gramps," Poppy murmured. "We haven't heard from you in ages. Care to say hello?"

Nothing.

"I vote we pass the time by necking," Rico said.

"I always have time for that," Poppy agreed, going into his arms.

His lips were almost touching hers when she sensed something and opened her eyes. She began to laugh.

"There he is."

Rico looked above them and couldn't dismiss the appearance with science. Like love, it was inexplicable, beautiful magic.

* * * * *

LET'S TALK

Romance

For exclusive extracts, competitions
and special offers, find us online:

Or get in touch on 0844 844 1351*

For all the latest titles coming soon,
visit millsandboon.co.uk/nextmonth

*Calls cost 7p per minute plus your phone company's price per
minute access charge

Want even more
ROMANCE?

Join our bookclub today!